'No woman ~~...~~ **again. No wom** ~~...~~

If Morgan was sensi ~~...~~
at that…

But Morgan, it appeared, was not sensible. 'Not all women are alike,' she said softly. 'One bad experience and you're turned off all women?'

'Not in the way you seem to think, Morgan Muir. I *like* women. I like the feel of a woman in my arms, a woman's soft body against mine. But I don't want a woman in my life. Ever again.'

'You're a stubborn man, Jason…you've decided that all women are like your ex-wife.'

'Prove to me that they're not,' he challenged.

'I'll prove it.'

'How?' He was intrigued.

'In the only way I know.'

And then, giving him no time to react, Morgan closed the distance between them.

Rosemary Carter was born in South Africa, but has lived in Canada for many years with her husband and her three children. Although her home is on the prairies, not far from the beautiful Rockies, she still retains her love of the South African Bushveld, which is why she likes to set her stories there. Both Rosemary and her husband enjoy concerts, theatre, opera and hiking in the mountains. Reading was always her passion, and led to her first attempts at writing stories herself.

COWBOY TO
THE ALTAR

BY
ROSEMARY CARTER

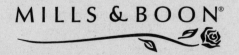

First published in Great Britain 1997
Harlequin Mills & Boon Limited,
Eton House, 18-24 Paradise Road, Richmond, Surrey TW9 1SR

© Rosemary Carter 1997

ISBN 0 263 80363 5

Set in Times Roman 10½ on 11¼ pt.
02-9709-51835 C1

Printed and bound in Great Britain
by Mackays of Chatham PLC, Chatham

CHAPTER ONE

'Who on earth can that be?'

Jason Delaney pushed back the broad brim of his stetson hat, his dark eyes narrowing at the sight of the vehicle that was approaching the ranch-house. The road was used mainly by pick-up trucks—a small car, like the one now coming through the trees, was a rarity.

The dog, following close on the heels of the broad-shouldered man, gave a token growl. Aging though Scot might be, he was not so old that he had forgotten that the ranch was his territory. Jason looked down at the big dog, who had once had no equal when it had come to working with cattle, and for a moment his eyes were troubled.

But this was not the time to think about the dog for the car was just stopping in front of the house. The driver's door opened, and a girl emerged.

A girl! Jason stiffened. It was a while since a female had been at the ranch.

The big dog growled and moved towards the girl.

'Scot!' Jason called a stern warning. 'Back, Scot.'

To his surprise, the girl said, 'Oh, that's OK, I'm not frightened.' And, bending towards the dog, she said, 'Aren't you lovely?' She stroked Scot between the ears, and the dog quietened in seconds.

The girl straightened. As she came towards him something tightened inside Jason. She was so light, so graceful—her movements made him think of a dancer.

'Hi, there,' she said with an enchanting smile.

'Hi,' he returned, looking down—quite a long way down—into the prettiest face he had ever seen.

5

Her hair was the colour of ripe corn, her eyes as blue as the Texas sky on a cloudless day. Her waist was so tiny that a man could circle it easily with his hands, and then have some space to spare. Through a cream shirt, tucked neatly into beautifully cut matching pants, a pair of small breasts hinted at promise and perfection.

After a long moment Jason said, 'Wasn't expecting company. Guess you're lost. Tell me where you're headed, and I'll give you directions.'

She had to tilt her head in order to look at him. 'Lost? I don't believe so. This is Six-Gate Corral, isn't it? I saw the name on the gate as I turned in.'

'Right—this is Six-Gate Corral.'

'Good! Then I've come to the right place. And I'm not company, exactly. I'm Morgan Muir.'

The way she said it was as if she expected him to know who she was. But the name meant nothing to him. Jason looked at her, puzzled.

'Morgan Muir,' she repeated. 'The new cook.'

'You have to be kidding!' The words exploded from his lips.

'Why would I do that? Look, Mr...' She stopped.

'Delaney. Jason Delaney.'

'*Jason Delaney*?' She looked amazed. '*Owner* of Six-Gate Corral?'

Jason nodded curtly. 'Owner, that's right.' His eyes were suddenly hard. 'I'm a busy man, Miss Muir. I don't have time for games.'

'Neither do I.' For the first time she looked angry. 'Look, I've done absolutely nothing to deserve your hostility.'

'OK, then, suppose you tell me why you're really here.'

'I did—I'm the new cook.'

'The hell you are!'

Her eyes sparkled as her hands curled into fists. Five

and a half feet of challenging woman. Quite a sight. 'I will not let you intimidate me, Mr Delaney.'

'Is that what I'm doing?'

'You're trying your best to. You have a cook by the name of Brent, don't you?' And when Jason nodded she went on, 'Off on vacation for a month, and in need of a substitute?'

An alarm bell rang in Jason's mind. 'How would you know that?' he asked aloofly.

She gave him a saucy look. 'Brent's ad appeared in a ranching magazine, and I happened to see it. I called him, we talked and he gave me the job.'

Jason frowned. 'I see.'

'Didn't he tell you?'

'No.'

'I guess it slipped his mind.'

Jason looked down at her, an enticingly fragile figure. Her eyes returned his look—wide, blue, confident. 'Anyway, Brent will be waiting for me. He'll want to tell me all about my duties.'

'Sure of that, are you?' Jason asked derisively.

'Of course.' Her eyes were challenging now. 'He must have told you *something* about me.'

'Only that he'd arranged for someone to take his place while he's on vacation.'

'Well, then!'

'Not a word about hiring a woman. Morgan…' Jason frowned. 'Now that I think of it, Brent did mention the name. But Morgan is a man's name, not a woman's.'

Morgan laughed, the sound making Jason think of music. 'It's one of those names that can belong to a man or a woman. Is Brent here, Mr Delaney? If he is, he'll be able to clear up this misunderstanding in a minute.'

'He'll certainly have some explaining to do,' Jason said grimly.

Turning away from Morgan, he shouted, '*Brent*!'

Minutes later a familiar figure came into view. Jason was in his early thirties; Brent was more than double that age—a weathered man with bow legs and skin like an old leather saddle which had been left out too long in the Texas heat. Like Jason, he wore boots and a stetson but his were more battered. In his hand was an ancient suitcase.

'You called me, Jason?' As his eyes fell on Morgan he stopped short. 'Miss Muir…' he said uneasily.

'Hi, Brent,' she said with a smile.

Jason stared from one face to the other in amazement. 'You really do know each other?'

A blue-eyed smile touched her face. 'Brent and I met in Austin—didn't we, Brent?'

'I don't believe it!' Jason exclaimed.

'You may as well,' the annoying girl said serenely.

Turning to Brent, she held out her hand to him. 'Nice to see you again.'

Shyly the old cowboy glanced at the proffered hand. Jason suppressed a smile as he wondered whether Brent would take it. He did—quickly, jerkily—in the manner of one who had had limited contact with women and was, in fact, a little scared of them. As if Morgan Muir were a being from another world—which, in a sense, she was, Jason thought in wry amusement.

Brent dropped Morgan's hand a second after touching it. Beneath the leathery tan his face was flushed. 'Be on my way now, Boss.'

'Not so fast, you old rogue,' cautioned his employer. 'Jason?'

'Who is this woman?'

Brent shot Morgan a quick look, before turning back to Jason. 'Miss Muir. Reckon she's the new cook.'

'New cook be damned! Why didn't you tell me?'

'I did, Boss. Told you I'd arranged a replacement.'

'You didn't say she was a woman.'

The old cowboy shifted his feet on the sun-baked ground. 'Maybe not,' he admitted at length. And then added hopefully, 'Did tell you her name, though. Positive I did.'

'Morgan. A man's name. Don't look so innocent, you old scoundrel; it won't wash with me. You know very well I thought the cook was a man.'

'Maybe so...'

'Well, then?' Jason was becoming more exasperated by the second. 'Why didn't you hire a man?'

'Couldn't get one,' Brent said simply.

'I should tell you not to come back, you old reprobate,' Jason growled.

Brent looked affronted. 'Only one answer to the ad,' he protested indignantly. 'Not as if I didn't *try* to find someone else.'

'Nice to know I was hired because I was the only option,' Morgan said wryly.

'We don't employ females at this ranch,' Jason told her crisply. 'I'm sorry there's been a mistake, but now that you understand the position I'm sure you'll want to leave.'

'No.'

'No?'

Looking down at Morgan, Jason saw an expression that he didn't quite trust. He hoped quite fervently that she would not take it into her pretty little head to cry. Tears would be absolutely the last straw.

But Morgan did not cry. 'No,' she said again, this time with a firmness that Jason would not have suspected in the circumstances. 'I will not leave.'

'Did employ a female once, Boss,' a treacherous Brent chose that moment to put in. 'Woman called Emily. Remember?'

Emily Lawson, a large, amiable woman. She had been the ranch cook before Brent. Mother of three cowboys and grandmother of a huge brood of children, Emily had adored ranches and cooking with almost equal passion. Besides preparing meals for the cowboys, she had advised them on their personal problems and rallied them when their spirits were low.

Emily Lawson and little Miss Morgan Muir were complete opposites: whereas the former had been an asset to the ranch, the latter could only be a nuisance and a threat. Jason did not have to analyse why this should be so; he knew it instinctively.

'Of course I remember Emily,' he said impatiently. 'She was different.'

'Wasn't a looker,' Brent agreed with a sly sideways grin. 'Plain as a tree-stump Emily was.'

Jason could have cheerfully throttled the man. Why bring Emily up now? Whose side was Brent on, anyway—Morgan Muir's or his?

His lips tightened ominously. 'Emily is not under discussion now. This won't do, Brent, and well you know it.'

'You'll do duty in the cookhouse, Boss?'

Once more Jason's anger exploded. 'The hell I will! If it weren't for the fact that you've been here since the day I was born I'd fire you on the spot.'

'I'll be on my way now, Boss.'

'You'll stay and cook until you find someone more—'

Morgan chose that moment to cut in. 'It doesn't matter whether Brent goes or stays. It doesn't even matter whether I cook or don't cook. It was agreed that I'd spend a month at Six-Gate Corral, and one way or another I intend doing just that.'

She spoke with a firmness that made Jason scowl. 'I've tried to make it clear that I can't have you here, Miss Muir.'

'I'll be staying all the same, Mr Delaney.' The eyes that met his were steady and unafraid.

'Not if I can help it, Miss Morgan.'

'I signed a contract.' Her gaze turned to Brent, who was looking both intrigued and uneasy at the same time. 'Tell him, Brent,' she urged. 'Tell Mr Delaney what I signed.'

'It's true,' the old cowboy muttered. 'She did sign a paper.'

'*Why*?' Jason demanded.

'Had to be sure she wouldn't let me down.'

'I would never do that,' Morgan assured Brent, before slanting a disturbingly winning smile at Jason. 'The contract protects Brent, and I get to work here for a month.'

Witch, Jason thought, scowling down at her from his six feet four. A very pretty little witch, to be sure. OK, more than pretty—*beautiful*, if the truth had to be told. But provocative as could be. Aware of her very considerable power over a man and not ashamed to use all the wiles at her disposal in order to get what she wanted.

And if a man's heart were trampled in the process, well, wouldn't that just be too bad? Little Miss Morgan Muir—presumably it was Miss—would have got what she wanted. That was all that counted with women, especially the pretty ones.

'I'll take a look at that contract,' he said tightly.

'Brent has his copy; mine is in the car,' Morgan told him sweetly. 'You can see it any time you like.'

'As soon as possible,' he informed her crisply over the sinking feeling in his chest. Even without seeing it, he knew already that the contract would be watertight.

Somehow he would have to find a way of getting rid of this girl. After Vera's defection he had made himself a promise never to get involved with a woman again. He now knew that he had never loved Vera—that the most he had ever felt for his ex-wife had been affection, and even that hadn't lasted long. He had been lonely when they'd met, and she had managed to convince him that they should be married. For the purpose she had employed several calculated tactics. Hindsight told him that he should have seen through her immediately, but the fact was that he hadn't.

This girl, this blue-eyed tiny-waisted Morgan Muir, could hurt a man badly. Hurt him far more deeply than Vera ever had. Just a few minutes in her company had been enough to tell him that. Why, already he had an urge—*an utterly insane urge*—to run his hands through the soft fair hair that curled so enticingly around her small head, to taste lips that looked sweet as fresh honey. Morgan Muir was dangerous. Contract or no contract, he had to find a way of getting rid of her. Quickly.

'I have every intention of staying,' she said, as if she had read his thoughts.

'We'll see about that.'

'My mind is made up, Mr Delaney.' Blue eyes flashed him a challenge.

A pair of cracked cowboy boots shifted once more on the hot dry earth, reminding Morgan and Jason of Brent's presence. For some reason, they had both forgotten him.

As they turned from each other and looked at the old cowboy he muttered, 'Guess I'll be seeing you a month from now, Boss.'

Without another word he shuffled away around the house.

Minutes later the sound of departing hooves had Morgan whirling around. A big horse was proceeding down the road she had just travelled—and on its back was Brent.

'He's gone!' she exclaimed.

Dark eyebrows lifted. 'Didn't you expect him to go?'

'Not so quickly.'

'I suspect he was ready to leave before you came.

That the horse was saddled and ready. That he was alarmed by your arrival and wished he'd left earlier.'

'You're intimating he didn't want to see me.'

'He knew he'd have to explain.'

'You've made that quite clear, Mr Delaney. Still, I didn't think he'd go without...'

'Without?' Jason prompted.

'Without explaining my duties. Showing me around...'

'If you're a woman of experience you must know your duties already.'

She shot him a saucy look. 'Obviously I'll cope. But Brent did say he'd show me around.'

'Just as obviously he's not going to.'

'I guess not...'

'Shouldn't matter, though, if you've worked before.' Jason knew that he sounded arrogant.

He had the satisfaction of seeing her look a little uncertain—as if his words had intimidated her. He hoped they had.

'Look,' she said, 'it's scorching out here. Do you think we could go on talking indoors?'

For a moment Jason hesitated. He didn't want Morgan Muir in his house, even for a short time; he didn't need her invading his privacy. Still, she did look hot. He gave a curt shrug and wondered if she would see the gesture as unwelcoming.

'Why not?' he said, and led her into the house—into a cool room, all white walls and rather basic low-slung furniture. The graceful figure struck an intensely feminine note against the very masculine background.

Jason's expression was hard. 'About your work experience—why do I get the feeling you haven't had any?'

Morgan had been looking around her. Now she looked back at him, her blue eyes steady. 'I've worked,' she said quietly, 'but it's true I don't have the kind of experience you're thinking of.'

'Don't tell me,' he countered sarcastically, 'you don't know a thing about cooking.'

This time it was Morgan's turn to hesitate. 'I've cooked.'

'On a ranch?'

'No...'

'Where, then? A hotel? A restaurant? For a crowd of hungry people?'

Again there was that hesitation, so slight that it might have escaped Jason's notice if he hadn't been watching for it. 'For myself—in my own kitchen.'

His eyes swept the reed-slender body. Suddenly he grinned. 'Bird's food?'

She danced him an answering grin. 'Bird's food? Heavens, no, since I'm not a bird. But if you're asking whether I've cooked for a horde of men then, no, I've never done that.'

Jason looked down into a face with which he could not find even one fault—every feature in it was lovely. 'But you did say you'd worked. Where? What kind of work?'

Her chin lifted, as if in challenge. 'Well, actually, I work in a big store, selling clothing. I also do some part-time modelling for the store.'

Jason was astounded. '*Modelling*?'

'Photographic.'

'Good grief!'

Her expression became even more challenging. 'Department store fliers. Glossy fashion magazines that the store puts out for its customers. That kind of thing.'

People everywhere would see her—in different poses, maybe wearing flimsy things. Men—looking at her pictures, imagining her... An ominous expression appeared in Jason's eyes as he wondered why that thought should bother him.

His lips tightened. 'So you're a model.'

'Part-time.' Morgan drew herself up. 'Your tone, Mr Delaney, sounds as if you think there's something wrong with modelling—there isn't.'

'You're as entitled to your opinion as I am to mine.' His words were clipped. 'I do need to know one thing— why are you here?'

'We've been over that. To cook.'

'You know as well as I do that's absurd. Models don't spend their time slaving in hot cookhouses.'

'It's what I want,' she insisted stubbornly. 'I'm prepared to work as hard as I have to. Do whatever it takes. You'll never hear me complain, Mr Delaney, and I'll do a good job.'

'What's this all about, Morgan?' He made himself use her first name.

Her eyes widened for a moment, as if he had surprised her. Then she said, 'When I saw that ranching magazine Brent's ad leaped at me.'

'You're making no sense.'

Her smile was enchanting. It would be so easy to be disarmed by it. Too easy.

'I can see it wouldn't make sense, at least not without an explanation. You see, Mr Delaney, for as long as I can remember I've had a dream. When I saw the ad for a replacement cook I felt as if it had been placed there especially for me to read. As if I'd been *meant* to see it. So much so that after I spoke to Brent on the phone I flew from San Francisco to Austin just for an interview.'

Jason stared at her in disbelief. 'You flew from California to Texas on the off chance that you might land yourself a temporary job?'

'That's right.'

'Sorry,' he said flatly, 'but I still don't understand.'

Morgan laughed. The man who stood just a foot or so away from her, clenching his hands to stop them from pulling her into his arms, thought that the sound was as sweet as rippling water.

'I don't blame you for not understanding. The thing is that for most of my life I've wanted to spend three or four weeks on a ranch.'

'That's a long time.'

'I wish it could be longer, but it's as much time as I can spare from my job. My real life is in the city.'

Real life… 'Of course,' Jason said flatly. 'Models don't ply their trade on ranches.' And then added, 'What kind of dream?'

'It's a long story and you don't want to hear it right now. But ever since I can remember I've had this desire to see the way cowboys work and live.'

Jason's expression was forbidding. 'I'll give you a tour.'

'No thanks.'

'I'll take you out on the range, drive you around in a Jeep. An hour or two and you'll see all you want.'

'I want a lot more than that.'

Exasperating woman. 'I suppose you think cowboys are exciting? I've a fair hand with a lariat—I'll do a few twirls.'

'Mr Delaney—'

'Rope a couple of steers.'

'You really don't understand.'

Jason was beginning to feel as if he was being caught in a trap with no way of getting out. 'What is it you want, Morgan Muir?' he asked harshly. 'Pointers on how to look your best in boots and a stetson? So that you can look the part when you model next year's collection of western gear? The kind of things women like you might *think* are authentic?'

'Why are you so bitter?' she asked him.

His lips tightened. 'Bitter?'

'Oh, yes. You seem to have such a low opinion of women, Mr Delaney. Or is it just me you don't like?' When he didn't answer she went on, 'Thanks for offering to show me around, but it's not what I want.'

'What *do* you want?'

'I keep telling you—a month on your ranch. I'll pay for the experience with my cooking.'

The walls of the trap were tightening. Jason frowned as he shoved his hands deep into the pockets of his jeans. 'I believe you know that you're trying my patience.'

Morgan's tone was light. 'Don't you think you're being a little unreasonable.'

Jason decided not to dignify the question with an answer.

He saw Morgan take a breath before she went on. 'I don't know why you're so opposed to me, Mr Delaney. Granted, I haven't had much experience as a cook, but I *will* learn and I'm not asking for favours. I saw an ad and I answered it. Brent could have asked me any questions he liked and I would have been honest with him. He didn't have to hire me—but he did, and he had his own reasons. So now I'm here. All I want is to spend a few weeks on your ranch, and I'm not asking for a free ride.'

'A model,' Jason said scornfully, his tone lashing her with the force of his contempt. 'Bet you don't know much about hard work.'

'If I were you, I wouldn't bet my last dollar on that.' Anger stirred in the lovely face, brightening blue eyes and staining soft cheeks with an appealing flush. 'You're obviously one of those people who think that modelling is all glamour. You're dead wrong, you know. It's hard work—gruelling.'

'Is that so?' Jason asked cynically.

'It certainly is! Some days, after hours behind the

counter and more hours in front of a camera, I'm so tired that I can't wait to get home. On days like that it's an effort just to gulp down a bit of food and make it to bed.'

'Sounds as if you don't enjoy your career.'

'Oh, but I do, Mr Delaney. I enjoy it very much. I'm just telling you that I do know about hard work. In fact, there are times when I'm tempted to...' She stopped.

'To what?' he prompted, interested despite himself.

'It doesn't matter,' Morgan said curtly. 'The fact is that I'm looking forward to cooking for your cowboys.'

'Morgan—'

'It's all part of the dream I was telling you about. Please...*please* don't take it away from me.'

There was something about her tone. Her expression. The passion with which she said the last words. Suddenly Jason was swept with a great wish to put his arms around Morgan and make life easier for her. To protect her. He took a step towards her.

In that moment he remembered Vera. She had breached his defences, and he had lived to regret it.

His tone turned to ice. 'You mentioned a contract.'

She seemed to be making an effort to control her emotion. 'Yes...'

'I need to see it.'

'Of course,' she said. 'I'll get it from the car.'

A few minutes later Morgan was handing Jason a folded envelope. As he took it from her his hand brushed against hers. In a second the wish to protect her turned into a strong desire to kiss her.

Wordlessly he looked at her. To his surprise, he saw that her lips were quivering. Their eyes clashed, dark eyes holding blue ones for an interminable moment. Then Morgan was stepping away from him, and Jason told himself that he was glad of the distance she had created.

He looked down at the envelope in his hand. When he looked up again his expression was sombre. 'All there, isn't it?' he said at last.

She was watching him intently. 'Sounds as if you're accusing me of something. What exactly do you mean, Mr Delaney?'

'You put in every damn clause you could possibly think of.'

'If there's something you want to say why don't you just say it?'

Jason gave a short, derisive laugh. 'Oh, come, Morgan Muir, don't look at me with those innocent blue eyes of yours. We both know who drew up this contract.'

Morgan seemed to be controlling her anger with some difficulty. 'You talk as if I've committed a crime. I haven't.'

'I take it you typed this.'

'Brent said he didn't know how. One of us had to do it.'

'If that was all there was to it. But you did more than type this, Miss Muir. These words…' Jason tapped the pages impatiently 'are not part of Brent's vocabulary. I doubt he could draw up a contract if his life depended on it.'

'I still don't know what I'm being accused of.'

'Getting what you want. In that, you're like—' Jason stopped abruptly.

'Like?' Morgan asked curiously.

Jason looked away from her. 'Someone I know.'

'A woman?'

'Not that it's your concern, but yes.'

An odd expression appeared in Morgan's eyes, one that Jason had not seen until now. He wished he knew what it meant.

After a moment she said, 'That's what I thought…from the way you spoke…' She paused. When she spoke again her tone was defensive. 'There's nothing wrong with the contract.'

'Except that you've ensured your stay at Six-Gate Corral for a month.'

'Sure I did. But the contract works two ways.' Morgan's voice was tight now. 'It's true that I made certain of my place at the ranch but, as I said earlier, we're both protected. Brent knows I'll be doing his work while he's gone—that I'll be taking care of things for him. That was important to him, knowing that the men would continue to eat well while he was away.' Blue eyes seemed to be asking for understanding.

Jason's gaze raked her face. 'I hope you're not expecting preferential treatment.'

Morgan tilted her chin up at him. 'Of course not!'

'Just so long as that's understood.'

'Absolutely.'

'You'll find the hours long.'

'No longer than the ones I'm used to working.'

'The heat will get to you.'

'I like heat.'

'Not the kind we get here,' he said grimly. 'You were wilting outdoors. You asked to go inside.'

'You have to admit it's a scorcher.'

'It is,' Jason admitted after a moment. 'The heat will get to you, nonetheless.'

'If it does it will be *my* problem, not yours.'

'And the dust.'

'I've been in other dusty places. Dust does wash off.'

She was spirited—he had to hand her that much. If what she said was true—the experience with Vera had taught him not to take a woman's words at face value—then she was certainly determined and fearless.

'You'll have to be up long before dawn to prepare breakfast.'

'When I'm modelling my day often starts at that time.'

He was running out of ways to put her off. 'If there's a round-up you could find yourself cooking out on the range, preparing food in a chuckwagon. You wouldn't find that much fun, Morgan Muir.'

'Oh, but I would! I'm longing to see a round-up! It's one of the reasons I'm here.'

Her eagerness startled him. 'You are?'

Morgan smiled at him, the kind of smile that had a way of shafting its way straight to a man's heart. 'Cooking in a chuckwagon—that's all part of the dream, part of the adventure. So stop trying to frighten me, Mr Delaney. Can't you see by now that I don't frighten so easily?'

Jason did see; he saw many things. But he still had a challenge left in him. 'Don't assume that the fact you're a woman—and a model—will carry any weight around here. The cowboys are concerned with cattle and horses; they don't know the first thing about fashion.'

'If they did I wouldn't be here.'

'I'm not interested in your career either.'

She shot him another one of those heart-melting smiles. 'I never thought you were.'

His eyes sparkled back at her, and for a second his lips curved in a grin. 'You'll be treated just like the men.'

'Haven't we been over that already?'

'I want to be sure you understand.'

'I do. Feel absolutely free to think of me as one of them.'

The suggestion was so absurd that he gave a shout of laughter. 'Difficult—when we both know you're not a man.'

'Mr Delaney—'

'That's one thing even you can't argue about, Morgan Muir—you are *not* a man.'

Once more he studied her, only this time his eyes went

from her face to her delectable body—skimming the line of her slender throat, lingering on the curve of soft breasts and descending to her waist and hips and thighs. When he looked up again he saw that her cheeks were flushed once more and her eyes stormy.

'I don't know how to convince you, Mr Delaney. True, I'm not a man, but nothing would please me more than if you treated me like one of the men. I wish you'd believe me. As far as you're concerned, I'm just one more ranch-hand.'

'Ranch-hands know they'll be fired if they don't perform satisfactorily. This contract...' Jason handed it back to her contemptuously '...doesn't protect you from that.'

Morgan gave him a cheeky grin. 'Thanks for the warning. I won't give you cause to fire me.'

Once more their eyes met. Then Jason glanced at his watch. 'The men will be returning from the range soon. They'll be hungry. Time to prepare your first meal, Morgan Muir.'

CHAPTER TWO

MORGAN had just finished making supper when the cowboys began to enter the cookhouse.

They came in singly and in little groups. They were tall, broad-shouldered men, with arms and chests that rippled with muscle. Men with faces that were deeply tanned, despite the stetsons they wore at all times, with far-seeing eyes—as if they were accustomed to looking across great distances. Attractive men, though not one of them was anywhere near as attractive as Jason Delaney. Morgan made the comparison without thinking.

She stood quite still for a moment as she remembered the quiver that had shot through her at her first sight of the ruggedly good-looking rancher. He was so handsome that he could have stepped straight out of a western movie—a gorgeous younger version of a tough Clint Eastwood—the good guy who could take on ten mean men single-handed and not be defeated.

She gave herself a small mental shake. So what if Jason Delaney was the most attractive man she had ever met? He was also impossibly autocratic and arrogant, and he had better not become her yardstick for all men. In fact, the less time she spent in the company of the man the better.

Almost to a man, the cowboys seemed amazed to find her standing at the long cookhouse table.

'Hi, I'm Morgan Muir,' she introduced herself. And when they continued to stare at her she elucidated, 'The new ranch cook. Didn't Brent tell you about me? Well, maybe not.'

They glanced at one another and then back at her, almost as if she were an alien being blown in by the hot Texas wind—as if they couldn't quite believe that she was real. Morgan reminded herself that they probably had little daily contact with women. She'd have to give them time to get used to her.

'I'm really looking forward to getting to know you all better.' She smiled, the unconsciously lovely smile that had affected Jason so strongly.

'Sure look forward to it, too, honey—sooner the better,' responded one of the men. He stood a little apart from the others, a man with a cruel face and lascivious eyes. She'd been wrong about this particular cowboy, Morgan realized. She'd have to watch out for him.

A moment later another cowboy said, 'Take it easy, Hank.'

'Don't need no warning from you, Charlie.'

'Take no notice of him,' Charlie advised Morgan. 'Glad to meet you, Miss Muir. All the men are. Welcome to Six-Gate Corral.' In contrast to Hank, Charlie had a gentle face and his smile was warm and welcoming.

At least she'd have one friend at the ranch, Morgan thought gratefully. 'Thanks, Charlie. Please don't call me Miss Muir, guys. I'm used to being called Morgan.' Her eyes swept over the men, all except Hank. 'I guess you're all pretty hungry after a day out on the range. Supper's ready.'

She had taken great care with the meal. The cook-house cupboards and freezers were well stocked with frozen foods, as well as with perishables. Without Brent to tell her what to prepare and reluctant to ask Jason, Morgan had planned the menu herself. Although she had never cooked for thirty men—a finger-foods party was more up her particular alley—she had always been re-sourceful.

Steak. The cowboys would like that, and there was loads of it in the freezers. Morgan had marinated the meat in a sauce made of lemon juice and spices, then broiled it and topped it with mushrooms. To accompany this were potatoes, halved and herbed and baked to perfection, a medley of carrots and peas and also a salad. And for dessert there was the frozen apple pie she had found in one of the freezers, warmed up to be served with ice cream. The cookhouse table was well scrubbed but bare. Morgan's final touch consisted of two glasses—she had been unable to find a vase—filled with wild grasses and placed at either end of the long table for decoration.

When the cowboys had seated themselves she put the platters of food on the table. Then she stood back, waiting while they helped themselves and eagerly anticipating their reaction to the meal she had set before them.

The reaction was not long in coming, only it was not the appreciative one that a bewildered Morgan had expected. The men did not take long to clear the platters. The complaints started when they asked for more food and discovered that there wasn't any. A rumble of discontent, begun by the obnoxious Hank and taken up by the others, became an uproar. Only Charlie refrained from taking part. He told Morgan that the food was delicious.

'Delicious be damned!' Hank roared. 'Are we men or a bunch of silly chickens?'

'Chickens!' Morgan defended herself indignantly. 'It's obvious you don't appreciate a good meal.'

'Call that a meal, lady? More like an appetizer.'

'Now, Hank,' Charlie said, 'Morgan tried.'

'Not enough, Charlie,' called one of the other cowboys. 'Not enough.'

'You're used to Brent's meals. I understand that.' Morgan struggled to make herself heard above the din.

'I'm truly sorry you didn't like the meal. Tell me what you want and I'll see you get it next time. All I ask is a bit of time.'

'We're hungry now, honey,' Hank sneered.

'Hungry now! Hungry now!' chorused the cowboys. 'Hungry now!'

Morgan pushed an unsteady hand through her hair. She was at the freezers, about to take out more steak, when a new voice—one ringing with authority—demanded, 'What's going on here?'

Morgan spun around as the noise in the cookhouse suddenly stilled. Tilting her head, she found herself looking into Jason Delaney's rugged, hard-boned face. Stressed though she was, Morgan found herself once again noticing shoulders that were impossibly wide and hips sexily narrow—a body that was lean and muscled.

'What are you doing here?' she asked.

'Came to see how you were getting on,' he said. 'Just as well I did, by the looks of it.'

'You should have seen what this dame tried to pass off as a meal, Boss,' Hank complained. 'Steak so small you could hardly see it.' He held up an enormous hand to demonstrate. 'Bits of potato with some kind of stuff stuck to them.' He pointed to the food which one of the cowboys had pushed away in disgust. 'Just take a look at this, Jason. We're men, Boss, not a bunch of half-weaned toddlers.'

'I liked it,' Charlie said.

'Charlie's appointed himself the lady's shining knight,' Hank said in disgust. 'Won't do, Boss. We've all had a hard day; we need to eat. Pretty lady here may make a man feel good at night, but she sure doesn't know what it takes to feed one.'

'Watch what you say, cowboy.' Morgan spoke with a firmness that not a few men would have had rueful cause to recognize, the same firmness with which she addressed men who tried to take liberties with her. Most of the time it was successful in keeping unwanted advances at bay.

Hank, however, was unabashed. 'Oh, yeah?' came the insolent drawl.

'You have a foul mouth, cowboy. I won't stand for it.'

'Oh, yeah?' Hank said again.

'That's enough,' Jason warned levelly.

'But—' Morgan said hotly, only to stop as a warning hand closed over her arm.

She was unprepared for the tingling that shot instantly from her wrist all the way up to her shoulder. But the touch did not last for seconds later Jason was turning back to the men.

'This is Morgan,' he said calmly. 'She's substituting for Brent. She means well but she's not familiar with our ways yet. Say, why don't you guys kick a ball around outside? We'll have some more dinner ready for you in a jiffy.'

To Morgan's surprise, the cowboys did as he suggested. Minutes later she could hear a ball-game starting near the cookhouse.

Jason's defence of her had been so unexpected that she said gratefully, 'Thanks for coming to my rescue.'

The rancher placed a pile of frozen steak to thaw in a huge microwave, before turning to her. Aloofly he said, 'I didn't do it for you.'

'I thought…' She broke off, dismayed at the hardness she saw in the ruggedly chiselled face. Not for the first time she wondered why Jason had taken such a dislike to her.

'Didn't fancy a mutiny on my hands,' he said drily.

'A mutiny?'

'You heard what Hank said—they're men and they're hungry.'

'I didn't cook enough and I'm sorry about that. But that Hank, he's crude and a big-mouth,' Morgan said hotly.

'He's also,' the rancher said, 'one of the finest cowboys on this ranch.'

'It doesn't bother you—the way he talks?'

'As I said, Hank is an excellent cowboy.' Jason's tone was abrupt. 'An expert at roping a steer or calming an excited horse.'

'That doesn't excuse his manners.'

'I don't hire men for their fine manners, Miss Muir.'

Her head jerked up. Morgan had never met a man like Jason Delaney—so sexy that her legs felt a little weak when she looked at him, and at the same time so cold and arrogant and contemptuous.

An unaccustomed wildness drove her to speak without thinking. 'Maybe that's because you don't have any manners yourself, Mr Delaney. You've been rude from the moment you set eyes on me.'

A hand shot out, grabbing Morgan's wrist and closing around it with fingers like iron. Dark eyes spoke volumes of contempt. 'If telling you that I disapprove of your presence at my ranch makes me rude then perhaps that's what I am. I didn't invite you here, Morgan. You're quite free to leave any time you like.'

Morgan tried to suppress the flames which were once more searing her arm, the sudden thudding of her heart and the treacherous, utterly unwelcome stirrings deep in her loins. 'You're forgetting the contract.'

Sparks flashed in Jason's eyes. 'Notwithstanding the contract.'

'I know you want to see me go,' she taunted.

He chose not to answer the taunt directly. 'You shouldn't have come in the first place—but you know that.'

'Brent wouldn't agree with you.'

'After the disastrous meal you produced?'

'Was it really so bad?' She tried to hide her distress.

Jason didn't answer her immediately. Tensely Morgan watched him at the microwave, taking out one lot of steak and putting in another.

When he looked back at Morgan his lips were tight. 'You saw the reaction of the men,' he said brusquely. 'Hank was right about one thing—the cowboys have been out on the range since dawn, sweating it out in the heat and the dust. Riding hard, working hard physically. They come back here, expecting a decent meal, and look what they got instead. They had every reason to be angry.'

'It was a mistake.' Her tone was low. 'I realize now that I didn't cook enough, but I did do my best.'

'You should have known, Morgan.'

'If Brent had stayed to explain…to show me around…' For some reason it was very important that this very dynamic man should think well of her.

'Any ranch cook worth his or her salt should know how to prepare a meal for a bunch of hungry men.' His tone was a shade dry. 'I wish I knew what you were thinking of when you applied for the job, Morgan.'

If only he were not so unyielding. Morgan swallowed hard. 'I told you, it's important to me…'

Jason put the thawed steak on the cookhouse grill, then opened a few huge cans of chili. Nobody would go hungry that night, after all.

He turned his head to look at her. A little roughly he said, 'It won't work out, you know.'

'You're wrong, it will!'

'I don't believe it, Morgan. If you're honest, neither do you.'

'But I do! And I mean to stay.'

'I think you should leave tomorrow.'

'Are you firing me?' Her voice shook.

Jason was quiet for a few seconds, and Morgan saw a little muscle move in his hard jaw. 'I don't have grounds to fire you,' he said at last, 'but I'm asking you to go.'

Morgan looked at him unhappily. 'I made a mistake,' she whispered. 'That's all it was. People have to learn.'

'There will be other mistakes.'

'Not if I can help it.'

'I don't see any point in waiting, Morgan.'

Suddenly Morgan was very angry. If she didn't fight Jason he would destroy her dream.

'I won't let you do this to me!' Her voice throbbed with passion. 'I deserve a chance.'

'Doesn't it mean anything to you that you're not wanted at this ranch?'

The words were like a hard blow in the stomach, but Morgan managed to hide her shock. Her chin lifted. 'Not a thing,' she lied.

She braced herself for Jason's next verbal assault but, oddly, he was silent. For a few seconds the only sounds in the cookhouse came from the sizzling of the meat and the loud ticking of the clock on the wall.

And then Jason's expression changed. Morgan saw his eyes going over her, and she drew in her breath. At twenty-two she was used to men. She was often photographed with male models, sometimes just posing with them, often with an arm slung around her shoulders and now and then a hint at something more amorous. Many a man had wanted to make love to her, inside as well as outside the confines of a studio, but she had never been interested. She had learned how to decline, politely but firmly, and still remain friends.

For some reason her reaction to this man was different. Morgan had never felt so disturbed and uncertain. Jason Delaney was undressing her with his eyes and she felt stripped and naked, acutely aware of the sparks which seemed to fill the air between them and conscious of his overwhelming maleness and of her own femininity.

'It really means nothing to you that you're not wanted?' he asked softly.

'I can only tell you that I intend to do my best.' Her voice was not quite steady.

In the dark eyes there was a flash of steel and once more that tic in his jaw. 'It won't be easy,' he warned.

'Maybe not.' The look she shot him was deliberately provocative. 'But I asked you earlier not to frighten me. Don't you understand that your scare tactics have no effect on me?'

After a long moment Jason smiled down at her. 'I'm beginning to understand,' he said.

It was a smile which made the anger leave Morgan. She looked at his dark eyes, his hard cheekbones and his sensuous lips—wondering inconsequentially how they would feel against hers—and knew that she had never met anyone as attractive as Jason. Her heart was beating so hard now that she made herself take a quick step away from him lest he heard it.

'Then you will let me have my chance?'

'I'll be watching you every moment.' Behind the smile lay a threat.

'I'll do my best,' she said again.

'Let's both hope it will be good enough.'

The steak was sizzling on the grill and the chili simmering in a huge pot when the cowboys filtered back into the cookhouse. They sat down at the long table and proceeded to eat, amazing Morgan with the extent of their appetites and the size of the portions they piled on their plates. She had not known that men could eat so much.

'They're cowboys, not male models watching their

figures.' Laughter glinted in Jason's eyes, as if he had guessed Morgan's thoughts.

She was awed. 'I had no idea.'

The glint intensified. 'You should know, Morgan, that Brent usually eats in the cookhouse with the men.'

A little taken aback at the thought of sitting down at the long table and partaking of the gargantuan meal, Morgan hastily shook her head. 'Tomorrow perhaps. I'm not hungry now.'

'Actually,' he said, 'I was going to tell you to eat with me.'

Morgan's head jerked. 'With you, Mr Delaney?'

His eyes sparkled at her expression. 'Since it seems we're going to be stuck with each other for a while, don't you think you should start calling me Jason?'

Jason... It was a nice name. Strong. For some reason Morgan looked forward to saying it when she was alone—when she could enjoy the sound of it on her tongue.

'Well, Morgan?' he asked.

'You don't eat with the cowboys?' The invitation—if it could be called that—had caught her completely off guard, and she had to say something.

'Brent usually cooks for me at the house.'

'In that case, I will too.'

'Brent cooked enough for a week before he left.' On a slightly softer note Jason added, 'You've been driving all day. You're probably exhausted.'

Jason Delaney showing a little human sympathy and friendliness? Miracles would never cease!

'Not too tired to do my job,' Morgan said spiritedly. 'And in case you're trying to trick me, Jason, forget it— I'm not about to fail another test.'

The tall rancher grinned, a daredevil grin that did alarming things to Morgan's senses. 'Neither a trick nor a test. I have enough for two so you might as well share it.'

With difficulty Morgan resisted the temptation to accept. 'I told you,' she managed, 'I'm not hungry.'

Jason laughed, the sound low and dangerous. 'As you like.' He made no further effort to persuade her.

When Morgan emerged from the cookhouse some time later there was no sign of Jason. Although it was still hot outside, the western sky was now tinged with pink and long shadows lay over the brushlands. On the hard-baked ground beyond the bunkhouse another ball-game was in progress. Morgan walked in the opposite direction: she had no desire for another unpleasant run-in with Hank.

She was frowning as she looked at the shadows all around her. For the first time since she had arrived at Six-Gate Corral she was wondering where she would spend the night. If her employer had been anyone but Jason Delaney, Morgan would have had no hesitation in asking him what to do, but Jason unnerved her to such an extent that she was reluctant to ask him the question.

Still, she had to sleep somewhere. The ranch-house was obviously off limits—she could not sleep in the same house as Jason—and if there was another suitable building she couldn't see it. Her car—of course! The thought came to her as she remembered that her suitcase was still in the boot.

But after just a few minutes in the car Morgan knew that she couldn't spend the night there. After standing in the sun for hours, the car was a hell-hole, hot as a furnace and airless—impossible to breathe in, let alone sleep.

Which left only one place. Morgan recoiled at the very thought of the bunkhouse. How on earth could she bear to sleep there? Sharing quarters with the ranch-hands—putting up with the ribaldries of a man like Hank. No, the bunkhouse was definitely out of the question!

There was nothing for it, after all, but to swallow her pride and speak to Jason. Somewhere there had to be an unused building, and he would have to let her use it.

But when Morgan knocked on the door of the ranch-house there was no answer. She walked around to the back, and there was no answer there either. There were no barking dogs and no sign of Jason's Jeep.

Boy, was she in trouble!

The words she had said to Jason earlier returned to haunt her now: 'Nothing would please me more than if you treated me like one of the men… As far as you're concerned, I'm just one more ranch-hand.'

They had been words spoken in the heat of the moment. And now look at the dilemma she was in!

The cowboys were still busy with their ball-game when Morgan, giving them a wide berth, carried her suitcase quickly into the bunkhouse.

Her heart sank as she took in the long room. It reminded her of a dormitory she had once occupied. Beds lined the walls, a cupboard and a bureau beside each one. At one end there was a television set and several chesterfields. The place was clean, even comfortable in its own way, but overwhelmingly masculine.

The thought of sleeping here was so appalling that it occurred to Morgan, for the first time, that Jason could be right. Perhaps, after all, she had no place at Six-Gate Corral. Perhaps she should leave first thing tomorrow.

And then she remembered her dream. *I'm here. A month at a ranch. A chance to realize my dream.* Seen in that light, it didn't seem to matter quite so much that she might have to spend the night in the bunkhouse. Her resolve stiffened.

In a dim corner at the far end of the room and at a

little distance from the other beds Morgan found one that looked as if it didn't belong to anyone. She shoved her case quickly beneath it, before climbing—still fully-clothed—between the sheets.

As she lay there, feeling more nervous by the second, new problems came to mind. What on earth was she going to do about dressing, about using the bathroom? But for every problem there had to be a solution. Morgan forced herself to think calmly. She would steal out of the bunkhouse very early in the morning, she decided, long before the men opened their eyes. The cookhouse had a bathroom. And tomorrow she would find some other place to sleep.

It was growing dark outside when the cowboys began to arrive back at the bunkhouse. Morgan lay quite still, the thin grey blanket pulled up to her chin and her breathing as shallow as she could make it—hoping against hope that no one would see her. And, in fact, no one did. They didn't even come near her bed.

Most of the men gathered around the television, where a baseball game was in progress. Baseball was evidently a favourite game at the ranch, and much debated. There were loud cheers when certain players did well and boos when they performed badly.

In her dark corner Morgan began to relax just a little. Tomorrow she would make other sleeping arrangements. For tonight, despite her doubts, this was going to be OK.

It was quite dark outside when a new voice was heard in the bunkhouse. Around the television the excited comments stilled.

'Morgan's missing,' Jason was saying. 'The new cook. Anyone see her?'

'Not since supper.' That was Charlie's voice.

'Pretty lady like her, we'd have noticed her around.' Hank was speaking. 'Maybe the cooking's too much for her and she's left the ranch.'

Listening to the comments, Morgan lay rigid. Her breathing was shallow, and in her stomach a hard knot of tension had formed. The one thing she had not considered was that Jason might come looking for her. It had been stupid of her perhaps, but there had been more pressing things to think about.

'She isn't in the cookhouse, but her car is where she left it.' Jason sounded strangely troubled. 'She's still on the ranch—somewhere.'

'Maybe she's in your bed, waiting for you,' Hank suggested.

'Cut it out!' an enraged Charlie shouted.

Jason ignored Hank's comment. 'Have to find her. It's dark now and she doesn't know her way around. I've searched everywhere I can think of. Only place I haven't looked is here.'

'The bunkhouse?' The baseball game was forgotten for the moment as the cowboys stared at their employer, amazed at the suggestion.

'Could she be in the bunkhouse, guys?' he asked. To a man, the cowboys said that wasn't possible but Jason persisted. 'Before we get out a search party, mind if I scout around?'

He found her minutes later, still trying to make herself invisible in the corner bed. For a long moment he stood scowling down at her, well over six feet of irate man—powerful, dangerous, infinitely intimidating.

'What the hell do you think you're doing?' he demanded at last. His voice was taut with anger, his face a furious mask.

'Jason…' she whispered, so nervous that she was shaking.

'Nothing but trouble from the moment you got here,' he snarled. 'Get out of that bed, Morgan, and be quick about it.'

'Jason,' she said again and stopped. By now the cow-boys were gathering around the bed.

Not surprisingly, Hank elbowed his way to the front. 'If it isn't the luscious Morgan,' he drawled.

'Leave her alone, Hank!' Charlie was there as well.

'Get lost, kiddo,' the big man snarled at him. 'She likes guys, don't you, honey?'

'That's enough, Hank,' a stony-faced Jason said. And to Morgan he added, 'Come with me.'

'Hey, Boss,' Hank protested, 'why don't you let the woman be? Seems to me she's after some fun. I'll see she gets it.'

'You heard me, Hank,' Jason warned, while beside him Charlie bristled.

Alarmed by the mounting tension, Morgan tried to calm the men. 'Jason, Charlie, you don't need to protect me. I can look after myself.' And to Hank she said, 'You won't lay a finger on me, cowboy, so why don't *you* get lost?'

The hard-faced man laughed unpleasantly. 'The pretty lady has spirit. This is going to be fun. I want to get to know you better, honey. Your bed or mine, and d'you want to wait till the rest of them are asleep or d'you want a good time now?'

'Enough, Hank,' Jason warned again, a note of anger etching the calmness of his tone.

'Hell, Boss, why not? This dame isn't a lady, and I believe she wants to get better acquainted.'

'Cut it out!' Charlie yelled.

At the same moment Jason rounded on Hank, his ex-pression savage. As two of the men held Hank back the others looked on disbelievingly. In the bunkhouse the level of tension was so intense that the air crackled.

A few seconds passed. And then slowly, deliber-ately—as if with an effort—Jason stepped back. Hank's exhalation of breath was audible. The men who had been holding him loosened their grip on his arms.

Jason turned to Morgan. 'You'll get out of that bed right now or I won't answer for the consequences.'

Mutely Morgan stared up at him, her eyes pleading with him to understand her dilemma. To get out of bed when all the cowboys were watching would be the ultimate in humiliation.

'Listen to me, Morgan.' Bending low over the bed with his lips almost touching her ear, Jason spoke in a voice that only she could hear. 'If you don't get out of bed right now I'll have to carry you. I don't have to tell you that all the men, but especially Hank, will love the entertainment.'

Morgan did not doubt that Jason meant what he said. He left her little choice. With all the dignity she was able to muster in a situation that did not allow for much dignity—and watched by thirty pairs of interested male eyes—she pushed aside the blanket and neatly swung her legs off the bed.

Jason picked up her suitcase and Morgan allowed him to take her arm and propel her through the group of men because she knew that it would do her no good—and probably a lot of harm—to protest. Charlie smiled at her as she was leaving the bunkhouse, and she smiled back. Hank's lecherous gaze she avoided.

'I'm perfectly capable of carrying my own case,' Morgan said when they were well away from the bunkhouse. 'Anyway, we're not going in the same direction.'

The remark earned her a furious look. 'I hope you're not thinking of going back there,' Jason snapped. 'Even you can't be as stupid as that. I won't come to your aid again, Morgan, and you can't expect Charlie to go on protecting you from Hank.'

'I was never in need of protection,' Morgan said.

'Really?' Jason's voice was quietly dangerous.

'Until you came looking for me the men had no idea I was there. Anyway, I'm not going to the bunkhouse, I'm going to my car.'

'You're leaving?' Jason's tone was odd and his eyes held an inexplicable expression of bleakness.

'That's what you'd like, isn't it?' Morgan threw the words at him bitterly.

'Is that what you think?' Jason asked enigmatically.

Looking up at him, Morgan was struck once more by an appearance that was all rugged toughness. The modelling part of her career brought her into the company of many attractive men. She remembered a man by the name of Casey who had striven for just this tough cowboy effect. But on Casey the stetson and boots, the carefully applied tan and the macho stance had looked contrived—perhaps because Casey was anything but a real cowboy. Jason was the genuine article. For a moment Morgan stared up at him, bemused.

'I haven't forgotten your warning,' she remarked. 'You said you'd be watching me every moment. I guess you feel free to fire me now. After all, you've been wanting me to go ever since you set eyes on me.'

'What I want isn't an issue right now.' Jason's jaw was inflexible.

Morgan was puzzled. 'What do you mean?'

'If you're thinking of leaving the ranch you've left it too late—for today, anyway. It's dark and you'd get lost long before you reached the highway.'

'And you don't want to be responsible if anything happens to me. Jason Delaney, owner of Six-Gate Corral, letting an irresponsible female loose at night on the lonely prairie. Wouldn't do your reputation much good, would it?'

'You really are the most provocative woman,' he said through clenched teeth. 'It will be good riddance when you do hit the road. And you're right—I don't want you on my conscience.'

'Actually,' Morgan said unhappily, 'I don't want to leave. Despite everything that's happened. I want to stay at Six-Gate Corral until Brent gets back.'

Jason stiffened—no doubt, Morgan thought wryly, because he realized that he was not to be rid of her after all.

'In that case,' he asked aloofly, 'why are you going to your car?'

Morgan looked up at him, and as usual she had to tilt her head. 'I have nowhere else to sleep.'

Jason was silent for several seconds. When he spoke at last his tone was unwilling, the words abrupt and hard—as if they were being dragged from him. 'There is a place—I took it for granted you knew that.'

Morgan looked at him hopefully. 'An outbuilding?'

'The ranch-house.'

'I will not sleep with you, Jason Delaney!' The words were out before Morgan realized how they would sound.

Jason's hands gripped her arms. They were big hands, and strong. Hands that would be able to rope a steer just as competently as the hands of any of the cowboys. Hands that would rouse a woman to unimaginable heights with the same ease. Morgan was suddenly burning hot.

'Don't remember inviting you to sleep with me,' Jason drawled sarcastically.

Morgan stared at him angrily. 'It wouldn't matter if you had. Either way the answer would have been the same.'

An eyebrow lifted. 'Fact is,' Jason went on drily, 'for several good reasons you can't sleep in the car—so the house is your only option. And I refuse—do you hear me, Morgan? I refuse to argue about it any more.'

In silence they made their way to the house. They

walked side by side yet apart, as if each was determined to keep a deliberate distance from the other.

As they went inside Morgan remembered her first impression of the house—that it would have been lovely if it had not been quite so spartan. It was tidy and spotlessly clean, but devoid of any personal touch. There were few pictures, no vases of flowers and not a single ornament.

When Jason had put down Morgan's suitcase in a guest room that was as neat and functional as the rest of the house he rounded on her. 'Suppose you tell me what you were doing in the bunkhouse?'

'I've already told you, I needed a place to sleep.'

'Don't remember telling you to go to the bunkhouse, Morgan.'

'You didn't, exactly—well, at least, not in so many words.'

One eyebrow lifted. 'You'd better explain since I'm not in the mood for riddles.'

The arrogance of his expression was annoying. 'You said I'd be treated just like the men.'

Jason stared at Morgan, before breaking into sudden and unexpected laughter. 'What I said was that you shouldn't expect special treatment.' The laughter stopped as his dark eyes studied her intently. 'I also said—' his voice was quiet now '—that it would be difficult to think of you as one of them.' His eyes were on her breasts and her hips. 'In fact,' he added drily, 'it would be impossible.'

The expression in Jason's eyes, that odd tone in his voice, made Morgan shiver. She tried to make herself ignore the feelings he awoke in her. She was already far too aware of his overwhelming masculinity—a quality that had as much to do with his superb build and looks as with his ever-present aura of strength and power. Jason was an implacable adversary, and it was imperative that she kept a clear head in all her dealings with him.

'Didn't it occur to you that you were humiliating me?' she demanded indignantly. 'Bossing me about in the bunkhouse. Demeaning me in front of the men—in front of that odious Hank. Threatening me.'

'You didn't get out of bed the first time I asked you.'

'Only because the cowboys were standing around, and I was waiting for them to move away. I didn't want a bunch of guys watching me. Besides, you didn't ask, Jason, you *ordered* me.'

'Have it your own way.' Jason was impatient now. 'We keep getting back to one fact. I didn't invite you to my ranch, Morgan. I wouldn't have let you have the job had I known about it. I can't help it if you look at a request as an order. I don't really care. One thing I do ask you to remember—I am boss here, and if you choose to stay I expect you to play by my rules.'

'I don't seem to have any other option,' Morgan said tensely. And then, because she couldn't help being interested, she asked, 'Would you really have carried me out of the bunkhouse?'

'You bet I would,' he told her crisply.

He stood not two feet from her, towering above her and radiating such a powerful aura of sexuality that Morgan's nerve endings felt raw. She ached with the longing to be swept up into those powerful arms and to feel the beat of his heart against her cheek.

Reluctant for Jason to read her emotions in her eyes, she forced herself to look away from him. Unsteadily she said, 'Despite anything you might think, I'd have been OK in the bunkhouse.'

'What makes you think that?'

'I've been around men. I can take care of myself.'

'You really believe you could have handled those cowboys?' he taunted.

'Sure. Why not?'

'I'll tell you why not.' Jason's voice was hard. 'They're a lusty lot. Women are a rarity out here, Morgan, and when they're about they attract attention.'

She knew what he was trying to tell her but his arrogance drove her to challenge him. 'I still believe I'd have coped.'

'Don't be so sure, woman. You've only been here a few hours and already there's tension on the ranch. You'd be blind if you hadn't noticed it. Hank, aggressive and on the prowl. Charlie, ready to protect you. Too ready. I won't have violence at Six-Gate Corral, Morgan. The odd spat is normal enough when you get a bunch of men, living and working together—especially tough men, as these are. But out-and-out fighting, alliances forming, one lot of men against another—that kind of thing leads to major trouble. I won't tolerate it, Morgan.'

'I don't like violence any more than you do, Jason.'

'Then let me warn you, if you insist on staying—and I'm asking you not to—sooner or later the men will come to blows over you.'

'I don't believe that,' she said heatedly. 'They won't fight because of me. I won't be doing anything to encourage them.'

'You can't help being yourself, Morgan. Hank won't change and Charlie will for ever defend what he thinks of as your honour, poor misguided fool.'

Morgan suppressed a shiver. 'Don't you think that in time the men will accept me as one of them?'

Jason gave a short laugh. 'How can they?' He studied her a few seconds in silence. When he went on his eyes were hard. 'You said you went to the bunkhouse because you needed a place to sleep. Was that the *only* reason, Morgan?'

'What other reason could I possibly have had?'

'That's what I'm wondering.' His tone was heavy with sarcasm.

It wasn't difficult to understand what he meant. Feeling a little ill, Morgan stared up into the ruggedly handsome face. 'Why do you dislike me so much, Jason?' she asked at last. 'To my knowledge, I've done nothing to offend you yet from the moment I came here you've shown me nothing but hostility. Why?'

Jason ignored the question. Instead he said relentlessly, 'Didn't it occur to you that your presence in the bunkhouse would be regarded as an invitation?'

'No—because I tried so hard not to be seen.' Her voice shook.

She saw the flash of steel in his dark eyes and the movement of muscle in his hard jaw. 'A woman in a bed meant for a man. Come on, Morgan, don't pretend you're naïve because I don't believe it for a moment.'

'Don't you care that you're insulting me, Jason?'

'Is that what I'm doing?' he jeered.

'Yes! How do you think the things you say make me feel?'

Brooding eyes ravaged her face. 'OK, Morgan, supposing you only went to the bunkhouse to sleep, what would you have done if one of the men had tried something? Really tried?'

'I'd have defended myself,' she said shortly. And when she saw the cynical look in his eyes she added, 'I thought I'd made that clear in the bunkhouse.'

'You spoke a few brave words. Don't suppose they meant anything.'

'Oh, but they did. Neither you nor Charlie would have had to help me, Jason. You see, I've been to a self-defence class.'

Jason grinned. 'Really?'

A second later she was in his arms. It happened so quickly that Morgan was taken by surprise. One moment they were facing each other across the little room and the next the strongest arms she had ever encountered were wrapped around her and Jason's mouth had fastened on hers.

His kiss was hard, so punishing in its onslaught that for a few seconds Morgan could scarcely breathe let alone think. It was half a minute at least before she remembered the self-defence course she had mentioned and had never had occasion to use. Another half-minute went by before she could think clearly enough to consider what move she should make. And by then the nature of Jason's kisses had changed.

They became softer and sweeter. There was a tenderness in them which made Morgan dizzy and numbed her thought processes. Sensations she had never experienced stirred in the very core of her being, setting her on fire with their intensity. The body against which she was welded was rock-hard, overwhelmingly masculine, making her feel deliciously feminine. Any thought of defending herself fled from her mind as she parted her lips in response to the demanding mouth over hers, and her fingers buried themselves in the hair at the nape of a corded neck.

When Jason lifted his mouth at last Morgan looked up at him in a daze.

'What happened to the self-defence skills?' he asked contemptuously.

'I…I was about to use them.'

'Right,' he said, and she knew that he knew she was lying.

Her cheeks were suddenly flushed. 'I could have.'

'Could you, Morgan? Maybe so. On the other hand, if brave intentions are the extent of your ability then I can tell you right now that you wouldn't stand a chance against a man like Hank.' He went on as she stared at him wordlessly. 'A word of advice, Morgan. If you don't know how to fight a fire, don't kindle flames.'

'You kindled them,' she accused.

'You didn't seem to object.'

Remembering the ardour of her response, she did not deny what he'd said. The heat in her cheeks intensified.

'Why did you do it?' she asked at last.

'You tell me, Morgan.'

She looked at him, still so shaken that it was a few seconds before she understood. Dully she said, 'To show me what could happen, I guess.'

An eyebrow rose insolently as Jason nodded.

'You had no right,' Morgan said through dry lips.

'I'm a plain man, Morgan, and I'm saying it as it is.' His eyes were sombre. 'You're in an all-male environment here, and you must know that there will be men who will want to touch you. When that happens I don't want you running to me with complaints.' He paused. When he went on his tone was measured. 'As for what happened just now—sure, I didn't ask permission to kiss you, but we both know you're as much to blame for the way things developed as I am.'

Morgan shook with anger. 'You'll never touch me again,' she seethed through clenched lips.

'I hope you're not expecting any promises from me.'

'I'm warning you, Jason, I'm the cook, not a…' momentarily she choked on the word '…not a concubine.'

Jason's laughter was deep and amused. 'A concubine on a Texas ranch. Isn't that a thought! I think you're scared, Morgan Muir.'

'Scared, Jason? Oh, no, just very angry.'

'You could leave.'

'Do you know how many times you've suggested that?'

'I'm suggesting it again. You could leave tomorrow as soon as the sun comes up.'

Morgan shook her head fiercely. 'What does it take to get through to you, Jason? I've come for a month, and I'm determined to stay.'

Morgan saw the way Jason's eyes swept her face, lingering on the lips he had just kissed. When he spoke again his tone was harsh. 'On your head be it, then, Morgan—if you stay you will have to accept any consequences.'

CHAPTER THREE

'THAT girl is trouble,' Jason said to the dog lying at the foot of his bed.

The only answer from Scot was a contented grunt.

'Major trouble.'

Staring at the star-studded sky beyond the uncurtained windows, Jason envied the dog its ability to sleep so peacefully. It was almost midnight, and so far there had been no sleep for Jason.

He knew precisely where to lay the blame for his sleeplessness. Damn Morgan Muir for intruding where she wasn't wanted, for making him feel things he had never felt before and did not want to feel.

Two sharp barks startled him out of his thoughts. Soft footsteps passed his door. Half a minute later he heard the kitchen door open and close.

By the time Jason entered the kitchen, Scot at his heels, Morgan was standing at the counter making herself a sandwich. At the sound of the door she whirled around.

'Jason!' she exclaimed. 'You startled me!'

He didn't answer but just stood there, looking at her.

'I thought you were asleep,' she muttered. 'I guess you heard the dog bark.'

He gave a curt nod but still no answer.

Morgan's expression was questioning. 'I didn't think you'd mind if I had something to eat...'

Mind if she took a bit of food? How much could a wisp of a girl like her possibly consume? For all he cared, she could empty the whole refrigerator—though he sensed that she wouldn't.

48

Hell, no, that was not what Jason minded. It was the sight of Morgan that got to him. In trousers and a shirt she had been tantalizing enough. But that thing she was wearing now! Looked like gossamer, the stuff that shimmered like jewels at early dawn, but even less substantial.

Shortie pyjamas, he supposed, for he had lived with a woman just long enough to know what some feminine apparel was called. They were pink and almost transparent so that he could make out the swell of Morgan's breasts through the thin fabric, and could even detect the hint of nipples. The panties were short, revealing the curve of a tiny bottom and a pair of legs that were long and smooth and supple. Legs that made a man ache to run his hand along the slim thighs, delicate calves and ankles.

Jason swallowed. Deep inside him a hard core of ice was beginning to melt. The knowledge gave him no joy. It made him angry and more determined than ever to remain on his guard against the female who had, against his will, invaded his domain.

'Mind?' He echoed the word curtly. 'Why on earth would I mind? There's more food where that came from. But I don't understand. I offered you a meal earlier.'

'I know…but I wasn't hungry then.'

'I believe you were standing on your dignity.'

Morgan threw him a cheeky grin. 'No.'

'I believe you'd made up your mind not to eat with me, and nothing was going to change it.'

'You appear to think you know what goes on in my head, Jason Delaney.'

Aloofly Jason stared down at this irritating slip of a girl who seemed to be doing her best to destroy the things he most valued—his solitude, his sense of being invulnerable and his resolve that women and emotion would never again be a part of his life. Morgan Muir was everything he loathed in a woman—independent, opinionated, determined—and if he was not very careful she might well succeed in turning his world upside down.

'You *don't* know my thoughts, Jason.'

Saucy wench. For the first time, and in spite of Jason's resolve, the ghost of a grin appeared in his face. 'I dare you to look me in the eye and tell me I'm wrong.'

Morgan lifted her chin at him. 'Well, OK, maybe you're partly right. But your invitation wasn't exactly friendly, Jason.'

'Friendly?' The grin intensified. 'What did you expect? A formal card, specially delivered?'

Blue eyes sparkled as she teased him back. 'Oh, yes, absolutely—gilt-edged and glossy.'

'Sorry to disappoint you, Morgan.'

They laughed together, and Jason thought how nice that was.

Then he asked, 'When was the last time you ate?'

Her brow wrinkled. 'Let's see…about fifteen hours ago, I think. I had a salad and a glass of milk before I got to the ranch.'

'That's it?' he asked disbelievingly.

'I stopped at a diner. Some place on the road. The food, mountains of it, didn't look very appetizing. As for the people…' She paused.

She didn't have to finish the sentence. Jason could well imagine the scene, the place and its patrons. A roadside diner where a hungry cowboy, a truck-driver or a man from the oil rigs could find a substantial meal. Mountains of food, as Morgan had just said, at reasonable prices. The men there would have been astounded at the sight of dainty Morgan Muir. They would have ogled her—with no bad intentions—and made her feel even more out of place than she already did.

'A salad and a glass of milk when everyone else was

devouring french fries and steak.' Jason laughed again.
Without thinking, he crossed the kitchen towards
Morgan and took her hands. Beneath his fingers her
bones were as fragile as a bird's.

Morgan looked up at him. Her mouth opened, as if
she was about to say something, but the words seemed
to die on her lips. Jason drew her closer. For a long
moment he held her, soft and almost unbearably fragile,
just inches from his own long hard body. He heard her
small hissing exhalation of breath. And then sanity returned, his grip on her hands loosened and he took a
step backwards—the distance between them once more
intact.

Wordlessly they stared at each other, the tension so
acute that it seemed to crackle in the air between them.

He had to say something, anything. 'The kettle's boiling.'

'Yes…' Her voice sounded a little unsteady. 'Like
some coffee, Jason?'

'Coffee…?'

He stared down at her, his expression harsh and a little
bleak. The light caught her hair, turning it to a dark gold,
and her eyelashes cast shadows over her cheeks. He was
still so close to her that a soft, sweet fragrance of some
kind filled his nostrils, making him feel a little dizzy.

Desire gripped him suddenly. In a sense Morgan had
been correct earlier when she'd accused him of kissing
her in order to prove something. There had been that, of
course. But there had come a point, very quickly, when
his motive had changed and when the embrace had been
all that had counted. Lost in the sweetness of Morgan's
lips, Jason could have gone on kissing her for ever. For-
tunately for him, sanity had returned and he had been
able to stop. What had shocked him had been how much
he had enjoyed those stolen kisses.

Now he longed to draw her to him once more—tightly

this time. He ached to feel the softness of her lovely body against his own, to crush her lips with his mouth. They were feelings he did not welcome, not with this particular girl—a girl who would be impossible to forget when she was gone.

'*Would* you like some coffee?' There was the strangest look in those blue eyes, as if she too was coping with some sort of emotion.

'No, thanks,' Jason said.

'Right…'

She went over to the kettle, unplugged it and filled a mug with coffee and a few drops of milk. It certainly hadn't taken her long to find her way around his kitchen.

'We eat breakfast early,' he said harshly.

She smiled at him. 'Of course. I know that.'

'Just thought I'd mention it. Life begins very early on a ranch and there will be ructions in the cookhouse if the men don't get a decent meal.'

'They'll have it,' Morgan promised.

'You'll have to be up by four,' Jason said, and wondered how two people could conduct such a mundane conversation when the air they breathed was charged with sexual energy and their minds were obviously not on what they were saying.

'I'll be up.'

'That being the case, the sooner you eat and get back to bed the better.'

'I told you, I'll have breakfast ready.'

'No excuses if you're late.'

Morgan's chin lifted to the challenge. 'I won't be late. I won't give you any reason to think you can fire me.'

God, but she was provocative! She knew only too well about the things he wanted to do with her. *Longed to do…* But he contented himself with saying tightly, 'See you in a few hours, then.'

Jason was at the door when Morgan said his name.

He turned his head. 'Yes?'

'I couldn't help wondering—who owns the perfumed sheets?'

He stiffened. 'The sheets?'

'Well, yes. This…' Morgan gestured about the kitchen. 'It's all a bit basic, isn't it? Almost spartan. The whole house is like that. Yet the sheets on my bed are perfumed and so pretty. They don't seem to fit in with everything else. That was why…'

Jason was stiff in an instant. Vera's sheets. It had never occurred to him that they were still in the guest room.

'Who owns the sheets, Jason?'

'My wife,' he said very distinctly and walked out, Scot leaving the kitchen with him.

Firmly Jason closed the door of his bedroom. As if he sensed something unusual, the dog gave a small bark. Jason ruffled the short hair between his ears and stroked the moist nose.

'That girl really is trouble,' Jason told his dog. 'If I'm not careful she'll turn my world inside out. Beats me if I know what to do about it.'

Even in bed, in the dark, he could still see Morgan. Try as he would, he could not seem to chase the image of her from his mind—the lovely face, the tantalizing figure. Morgan had known how close he had come to kissing her again, he was sure of it.

'She has to leave,' he said to the dog, who was already half-asleep at the foot of the bed. 'Even if I have to break her spirit with the hardness of the work, somehow I have to get her to leave this ranch.'

He heard the kitchen door close. As quiet footsteps passed the door the dog stirred but did not bark. For a woman who had had no more than a salad and milk in the last fifteen hours, Morgan had not taken long to eat, Jason thought.

*　　*　　*

Actually, Morgan had barely eaten at all. Jason's last words had left her stunned. *A wife!* Why had it not occurred to her that he might be married? As she crept between the perfumed sheets she wished that she didn't feel quite so sad.

She groaned when the alarm clock shrilled. It didn't seem more than a few minutes since she had gone to bed. She lay still for a few seconds, before forcing herself to open her eyes. It was dark in the room and the glowing dial by her bed showed that it was not quite four o'clock.

Four o'clock—and a bunch of cowboys hungry for their breakfast, before going out on the range. *Four o'clock...* It was inhumane!

Ten minutes later, dressed in jeans and a sweatshirt, Morgan was in the cookhouse. Jason arrived soon afterwards.

His eyes flicked her face. 'Made it,' he commented.

Morgan darted him a saucy grin. 'With time to spare. Bet you didn't think you'd find me here.'

Jason grinned. 'I admit to having had some doubts.'

'What would you have done if I'd overslept? Carried me out of bed and dumped me in the cookhouse—or fired me on the spot?'

'First the one, failing the success of which the other,' he told her crisply, but she saw the sparkle in his eyes.

When Jason wasn't being hostile he was dynamic, Morgan thought. Oh, but it would be so easy to fall in love with this man. It was a few seconds before she remembered why she had been so sad in the moments before she had fallen asleep. Jason was married. The smile left her eyes.

'Do you eat breakfast with the men?' she asked, more subdued now.

'Not as a rule.'

'You have your breakfast in the ranch-house?'

'Coffee, toast and a couple of eggs. Sometimes some steak as well. Brent cooks it when he's finished here.' Jason looked at Morgan. 'I don't expect you to cook for me, though. I told you that yesterday.'

Where was his wife? Did she never eat with her man? 'I'll do it all the same,' she said quietly.

'Glutton for extra work?'

'Just making certain I do everything Brent hired me to do.'

'I'm perfectly capable of making my own breakfast, Morgan.'

'I'm sure you're very capable,' she said stubbornly, 'but if Brent does your cooking I'll do the same.'

'What's wrong with you, Morgan? Are you totally incapable of taking a hint?'

'A hint, Jason?'

'Isn't it enough that I've had to let you sleep in the ranch-house?'

'Let me remind you that wasn't *my* choice.'

'And let me remind *you* that there was no other option,' he said grimly.

'Nice to know I'm so welcome,' she said sweetly.

'Having you constantly underfoot is just too much, Morgan.'

Morgan managed to keep any emotion from showing in her face. Jason Delaney would be only too pleased if he knew how much he was hurting her.

'I'll stay out of your way as much as I can,' she informed him crisply.

Would cooking also include making meals for Jason's as-yet-invisible wife? It was a silly question, of course, since Brent obviously cooked for them both. As Morgan began to work she wondered when she would meet Jason's wife.

At least this morning Morgan did not have to be told about the appetites of cowboys at the start of a long working day. She knew that Jason was watching as she went to work, preparing great mounds of bacon and steak, huge platters of scrambled eggs and enormous pan-cakes. It did not take her long to get the coffee going in the big urns and to lay the long cookhouse table.

By the time the first of the cowboys appeared in the cookhouse the place was full of tantalizing aromas and the meal was tastefully set out, ready for the men to help themselves.

Hank arrived, his demeanour making it obvious that he was once more ready to provoke her, but Morgan treated him with an offhand politeness that precluded lewd comments. And then there was Charlie his eyes lighting up at sight of Morgan, eager to sit close to her and bristling any time Hank was aggressive. Morgan liked Charlie. She also knew that he could prove to be an embarrassment in the long run, and she made a point of behaving towards him with a gentle friendliness that was just impersonal enough to put distance between them.

There were the other cowboys, with faces she recognized from the previous day. Big men, tough, ready to do a man's arduous work in the heat and dust of the brush. She couldn't help warming to them, attractive men all of them. They sat down to the meal with obvious gusto—not a single complaint this time—and Morgan felt a glow of achievement.

When the cowboys had finished eating Morgan decided to leave the cleaning up until later, and accompanied Jason to the ranch-house.

'I told you I'd make my own breakfast,' he growled.

'And I told you I was going to do the job for which I was hired.'

'You're an impossible female, Morgan Muir.'

'You could be right,' she said cheerfully.

Jason scowled at her. Then the tension left his face

and he grinned at her instead. He had an attractive grin—
Morgan had noticed that previously—that warmed his
dark eyes and settled easily into the lines around them.
His teeth were white and strong between a pair of disturbingly sensuous lips.

'If you're really insistent on making my breakfast—
not that I understand why you'd want the extra work—
you may as well eat with me.' He paused a moment. 'Or
are you going to refuse me again?'

'No, I think I'd like that.'

If Jason's wife was at the ranch she didn't make an
appearance in the kitchen and he didn't mention her.
They ate together in silence, but it was a relaxed silence.
Soon afterwards Jason picked up his stetson and left the
house.

Standing at a front window, Morgan watched him
walk to his Jeep—a giant of a man, striding powerfully
through the early dawn. Once he turned his head. Without thinking, Morgan lifted a hand in a wave. She didn't
know if he saw it, though he seemed to hesitate a moment. Then he was walking once more, his long legs
encased in hand-tooled boots and his long muscled arms
swinging at his sides. A man among men, at ease in his
terrain the ranch property covering thousands of acres.
Something stirred in Morgan at the sight.

'You said a dream brought you to the ranch,' Jason said
that evening when they were drinking coffee after supper.

There was still no sign of his wife. By now it was
obvious to Morgan that Mrs Delaney was not at the
ranch, but so far there had been no explanation for her
absence.

'A dream, yes,' she said.

'What kind of dream, Morgan?'

She smiled at him over her cup. 'It's a long story.'

'I have time to hear it.'

Morgan took a sip of the hot strong coffee, and for a moment her eyes seemed to turn inward as if she was remembering something. At length she looked at Jason.

'My grandfather was a cowboy,' she told him.

'A cowboy?' Jason repeated, immediately intrigued.

'He rode in rodeos and worked on various ranches. In hospital after a rodeo accident he met a nurse—my grandmother. They had one daughter, and she had me. Mom married an engineer, and my parents moved to California shortly after I was born. I didn't know my grandfather really well until after my parents were killed in a motor accident. My grandmother was no longer alive either by then, and it was left to my grandfather to look after me.'

'How old were you?'

'Just turned eleven.'

'An old cowboy and a young city lass,' Jason commented wryly.

'I can see you think that's odd—well, there were others who did too.' Morgan smiled softly, as if at her memories. 'It couldn't have been easy for my grandfather to raise a child on his own, but somehow he managed. He had retired from the ranching life by then and, although it couldn't have been what he really wanted, he decided that it was in my best interests to live in California.'

'Quite a change that must have been for him.'

'A change and a sacrifice,' Morgan said quietly. 'I don't think he ever really got used to San Francisco, with its traffic and the crowds of people. He used to long quite desperately for the quiet of the prairies. But he had his memories and his stories. Night after night he'd tell them to me. Stories about the ranches he'd worked on, the cowboys who'd been his pals. The bad times and the good. So many stories, eventually I knew most of them by heart.'

'Where is your grandfather now, Morgan?'

'He died,' she said simply. 'Just over a year ago. Very suddenly. So suddenly that I didn't even have time to say goodbye.'

She paused, and Jason saw the shimmer of tears in the lovely sky-blue eyes. After a moment she swallowed hard, and he saw her blink the tears away. It was another moment or two before she was able to continue.

'For me, his death was a terrible loss. At first I didn't know how I'd ever get over it. But I remembered all those wonderful stories, and eventually I knew that I had to go to a ranch and see for myself the things my grandfather used to tell me about. So there you have my dream, Jason. Nothing very exciting or dramatic. Just a great wish to spend a month on a ranch. To see and learn and experience. To make some sense of all the things my grandfather told me about.'

Her story was a simple one yet, for some reason, it moved Jason immensely. Not just the story, but the way Morgan told it—her voice, the words she used, the expression in her eyes as she remembered.

Jason was appalled when he realized how much Morgan was affecting his emotions. He didn't want to feel any of the things she was making him feel: the constant urge to pull her into his arms, to kiss her until there was no breath left in either his lungs or in hers; admiration for her stubborn persistence and her willingness to work in strange and difficult conditions; and the pleasure he experienced when he listened to her talk.

If he had sensed yesterday that Morgan Muir was trouble then today he knew it for certain. She was far more dangerous than Vera had ever been for she seemed to know just how to burrow her way into a man's being—to invade his heart and his thoughts. She was braver, more independent and eager than Vera had ever been because Vera had only been imitating those qualities. At the same time Morgan had a vulnerability that made a man long to protect her, to cherish her...

Jason could almost...*almost*...imagine living with Morgan. And that was crazy. *Insane*! He'd had one very bad experience with a woman who'd found ranching boring. There was nothing at Six-Gate Corral that could possibly appeal in the long term to a girl whose career was selling and modelling fancy clothes. She would laugh her pretty little head right off those sexy shoulders if she knew that he felt weak at the knees every time he looked at her.

Abruptly he said, 'It's all very well that your grandfather lived with his memories but it's obvious that he only told you the good things. Ranch life isn't all romance and fun, Morgan.'

She looked hurt. 'Do you think I don't know that? And you're wrong if you think my grandfather romanticized his memories. He told me so much.'

'I can just imagine,' Jason said harshly. 'I bet I can catalogue everything he told you. The drama of a round-up. The excitement of a rodeo. The sound of a guitar at sunset.'

'Those things—and so much more,' Morgan said softly. 'Yes, Jason, my grandfather told me about branding and round-ups. He made them sound exciting, but he also told me of the toll a round-up can take on beasts and men. He told me about the vastness of Texas and the wonder of the open spaces. About ranches covering hundreds of thousands of acres and about the flowers that come up in the prairies in the spring. The camaraderie and the loyalty of the cowboys.'

'As I said, he only told you the good things.' His voice still held that inexplicably harsh tone.

'Not only the good things, Jason,' Morgan said after a moment. 'Grandfather also told me about floods and cattle thieves. About calves lost or injured and needing to be rescued. He told me about the menace of the mesquite, those awful trees which are so difficult to get rid of with their sharp branches that can slash the leg of a man or a horse. He told me about the heat and the wind and the dust. And the loneliness.'

Jason was quiet for a while after Morgan had finished speaking. At length he said, 'You can see a ranch in a day. Two or three days at the most.'

Morgan shook her head. 'If that was all I wanted I could have taken a vacation some place where they take in paying guests.'

He had to convince her, Jason thought desperately. Get it into her lovely head that she did not need a month at Six-Gate Corral in order to relive her grandfather's experiences. He had to find some way of getting her out of his life quickly—before it was too late.

'I'll show you around,' he offered calmly. 'Now that I have an idea of what you're after, I'll show you everything. You can see the lot in a few days.'

'No, Jason.'

'No need for you to cook for the men. To get up before dawn and slave over a stove at night. A girl like you—that isn't what you're used to, or what you want.'

'It may not be what I'm used to, but it's exactly what I want,' she said with that heart-melting smile of hers.

'I don't think you understand how difficult the month will be,' Jason said grimly.

'I do understand that you don't want me here.' The blue eyes sparkled; the cheeks had a dimple which came and went in the most enchanting way.

'You're right about that. I *don't* want you,' Jason said, and knew that he was lying.

'That's too bad because I'll be here all the same. D'you know, Jason, the day I saw Brent's ad it was as if a prayer had been answered. I've taken leave from my job, and a friend is staying in my apartment for the month.' The sparkle in her eyes intensified. 'I'm sorry it isn't what you want, Jason, but think of it this way— a month is all it will be. You'll be rid of me after that. A month isn't very long. When it ends Brent will be back and you'll be able to forget I was ever here.'

There was no telling how much harm Morgan could do in a month. Jason's lips tightened. Alluring little minx that she was, men would be drawn to Morgan like bees to honey. It would take a mighty strong man not to melt when he looked at her. Sexy little witch, she would have had men eager to do her will from the time she'd understood the beguiling power of her smile. As for forgetting her—Jason knew he would not be able to do that.

Aloofly he said, 'When the month is over, Morgan, you won't find an excuse to stay here longer?'

She shook her head. 'Of course not.'

'Of course not,' Jason echoed harshly. 'You'll be raring to go by then. Ready once more for the soft life. A month is as much as a girl like you could ever take.'

'I...I'm not sure what you're saying, Jason.'

Actually, he was saying things he didn't want to say, but something drove him on anyway. He forced scorn into his voice. 'A girl like you could never be happy on a ranch for long.'

For a long moment there was silence, a silence filled with tension. As Jason waited for Morgan to reply he held his breath.

At length Morgan said, a little dully, 'A month will be just about the right amount of time. You won't have to worry that I'll try and stay longer than that.'

'Fine.' Jason's tone was flat.

For a while after that neither of them spoke. The coffee had turned cold but Jason drank it anyway. Morgan took a few sips from her cup too. The dog's panting was the only sound in an otherwise silent room.

'Do you ride?' Jason asked at length.

Morgan's head lifted. 'I've been on a horse. The store did a photo-shoot once, featuring riding clothes.'

'That wasn't what I asked, Morgan. Do you ride?'

'Not properly.'

'I find that hard to understand.' His tone was derisive, his way of hiding the emotions that the last few minutes had evoked. 'Your grandfather was a cowboy, and he never taught you to ride?'

'I told you about the rodeo accident. It was quite bad, Jason; he could never ride again after that. In fact, he could barely walk. He missed his horses terribly. I asked him sometimes why he didn't just go out to a farm and spend some time around the stables, but he could never bring himself to do that.'

Jason could sympathize with the old cowboy. 'If he saw a horse he had to ride it.'

'Yes. Even then...' Morgan stopped.

'Even then?' Jason prompted.

'I was longing to ride, and Grandfather did say he would teach me. But his heart wasn't in it, not when he'd have to watch me from the ground. And in the end illness caught up with him first.'

'I'll have to teach you, then,' Jason said.

Her eyes shone. 'You'd do that?'

'The only way to see a ranch—to see it properly—is on horseback. I take it you do want to learn, Morgan?'

'Oh, yes!' The elfin face was radiant. 'I'd love to ride.'

Jason felt a familiar melting sensation deep inside him. He would regret this, he knew, but he'd gone too far now to turn back. 'Have to fit you out,' he said gruffly.

'Jeans will be OK, won't they?'

'You'll need some boots. And a hat. Without a decent hat you won't last five minutes in the sun.'

'Is there some place nearby where I could buy those things?'

'There are things at the ranch you can use.'

A little of the glow vanished from Morgan's face. 'Your wife's?'

'Vera's,' Jason agreed curtly.

In a back room of the ranch-house, thrust deep into a cupboard, was a set of riding gear bought new in Austin at a time when Vera, then his ardent fiancée, had told Jason how much she wanted to ride…to be part of the ranch…to be part of his life. Her enthusiasm hadn't lasted two weeks beyond their wedding. Only then had Jason learned that Vera hated horses. Not only horses, but almost everything about Six-Gate Corral. He had no real reason to believe that when it came down to it Morgan Muir would be any different, he thought grimly.

'Talking of your wife,' Morgan said brightly, 'I haven't met her yet.' She paused a moment but when Jason didn't speak she went on, 'I take it she's not at the ranch right now, Jason?'

'You could say that.'

'Will she mind when she finds out I've been staying here?'

'Why should she?' The words were hard and clipped.

Blue eyes met brown. 'I know I'd mind if a woman was living with my husband.'

'We're not living together!' he lashed out. 'Didn't we establish that yesterday? We're sharing a house, Morgan. Nothing more to the arrangement than that.'

'Right.'

A fleeting expression came and went in the lovely blue eyes. Jason wished he knew what it meant.

'And yet,' Morgan said, 'if I were Vera I'd mind all the same.'

Jason's eyes were on Morgan's face, searching it intently now. It was a few seconds before he said, 'Vera and I are no longer together.'

Morgan stared at him. 'Are...are you divorced?'

'Yes.'

'You spoke of her as your wife...'

Jason thought he must have imagined the sudden sparkle in the blue eyes. 'You asked about the owner of the perfumed sheets and the riding gear, and I told you who they'd belonged to. It didn't occur to me to go into specifics.'

If there had been a sparkle it was gone now. 'Divorce is never easy,' Morgan said quietly.

'Speaking from experience?'

'Oh, no, I've never been married. I'm sorry about your wife, Jason.'

'Don't be.' His tone was brusque. 'It's better this way. Vera is happier in Austin than she ever was at Six-Gate Corral. Anyway, she has a new man in her life.'

'You must be lonely,' she said slowly, softly.

Her tone, the touch of sympathy, made him angry. 'Don't you believe it,' he said harshly.

'You're surrounded by the cowboys, I know, and they're fine men, all of them. Even Hank, in his own way, I guess. But still...' Morgan stopped.

Jason knew what she had been about to say. 'You assume I miss having a woman around.'

'Do you?'

'Not for a moment,' he said flatly.

'Jason—'

'Women cause problems. I've learned that to my cost. I have all I want, Morgan. The ranch, the animals. Freedom. Comradeship—undemanding comradeship—any time I want it. I don't need anything else.'

'I have a feeling you're trying to warn me about something,' Morgan said.

She was sharp, this girl. Well, perhaps that was good.

It would put them both on the proper footing. There'd be no misunderstandings when the time came for her to leave the ranch.

'A warning?' he shot back. 'Well, yes, maybe you're right. Understand, Morgan—Vera only married me for what she thought she could get from me. For a while she actually made me believe that she loved me, that she liked the idea of living on a ranch.'

'Things changed?'

'With a vengeance,' Jason said grimly. 'From one day to the next the ranch became a horrible place in Vera's eyes. Lonely, uncivilized, too isolated. She wanted to change everything. She littered the house with silly things—you should have seen some of her mementos and ornaments. What she didn't take with her when she left I got rid of. Everything, except the riding gear and those darned perfumed sheets—I'd forgotten they were there until you arrived.'

'Was it so bad that Vera wanted to do a bit of decorating?'

'Not in itself. The place could have done with some brightening up. No, that was just one thing. Vera wanted to change everything about me—about our lives. She actually thought she could get me to leave the ranch.'

'No!' Morgan exclaimed incredulously.

'She wanted us to live in a city, some place like Dallas or Austin, where she could shop and entertain and have dozens of friends while I ran the ranch from a distance. As if I were some bloody gentleman farmer.'

'You couldn't reach a compromise?'

'No.' Jason gave her the scornful look that the ridiculous question deserved. 'When Vera realized that she couldn't have what she wanted she sulked for a while. Then she left.'

Morgan hesitated a moment before saying, 'And you were hurt.'

'Yes… I tried reasoning with her, but without success. She left the ranch and quickly found herself another man, someone more to her taste.'

'You're very bitter,' Morgan said after a moment.

'Bitter?' Jason's lips tightened. 'I'd call myself realistic. Vera was only faking affection, and for a while I was taken in by her.' His voice changed, becoming flat and decisive. 'No woman will ever hurt me again. No woman, Morgan.'

Would Morgan heed the warning? Would she realize that he'd had enough of her sympathy and her questions? Didn't she understand that he'd had enough of her company and wanted nothing more than to see her gone? If Morgan was sensible she would leave things at that and refrain from saying another word.

But Morgan, it appeared, was not sensible. 'Not all women are alike,' she said softly.

'They are to me. I've yet to meet one who's different.'

'One bad experience and you're turned off all women?'

Jason looked at her, his expression aloof. 'Not in the way you seem to think, Morgan Muir. And I hope you're aware that you're really pushing the limits of this conversation. I'm as normal as the next man. I *like* women. I like the feel of a woman in my arms, a woman's soft body against mine. I like all that very much. But I don't want a woman in my life. Ever again.'

'You're not giving women a chance. You're a stubborn man, Jason, and you've decided that all women are like Vera.'

'Prove to me that they're not,' he challenged.

She stared at him, her face so transparent that Jason sensed a mixture of emotions raging inside her—anger, excitement, a strange wildness. Her cheeks were flushed, her eyes sparkled. Desires that no other woman had ever been able to wake in Jason surged in him now. Looking at the fragile girl with the flushed elfin face, Jason realized that all he wanted was to hold her in his arms and never let her go.

'I'll prove it,' she said softly.

'How?' He was intrigued.

'In the only way I know.'

And then, giving him no time to react, Morgan closed the distance between them. Jason was still seated as she bent over him and put her lips against his.

He was rigid in an instant, his body burning and pulsing. She was about to move away when he pulled her down. Evidently it was the one thing Morgan had not expected for she fell against him, sprawling over his lap.

And then *he* was kissing *her*. Hard, passionately—more passionately than he had ever kissed any woman. His arms held her soft body, his hands moving over her and exploring her. Every nerve, every fibre clamoured for total fulfillment, yet at the same time he was also aware of a need for restraint.

Eventually he lifted his head, his lips parting from hers for what he intended to be no more than a second. Morgan took the moment to tilt back her own head so that she could look at him. She was so close to him that he could see the lights that warmed her eyes and the damp tendrils of hair on her forehead.

'What was that all about?' she whispered.

'You can ask me that?' he taunted.

'I don't understand…'

'Come on, Morgan. You started it.'

'All I did was kiss you. Very lightly.'

'To prove that women aren't all the same.'

'That's right… I didn't expect such a violent reaction.'

'What did you expect?' he persisted.

'Not…not what just happened.'

'You should know, Morgan—' Jason's tone was measured now '—that when you set out to seduce a man you should always be ready for anything. The script won't necessarily run the way you picture it.'

'I didn't have a script, nor did I try to seduce you.'

Her cheeks were hot, her eyes shocked. What a good actress she was, Jason thought grimly. Even Vera had never been quite so convincing.

'Didn't you?' he jeered.

'No!' Morgan exclaimed indignantly. 'Just the opposite. I was trying to prove to you that women aren't only out to scheme and manipulate. I was showing you some affection.'

'Affection,' Jason said mockingly. 'Is that what it's called these days?'

He made to draw her closer against him once more but Morgan resisted him. Deliberately she levered herself out of his lap. She didn't go back to her chair but stood, looking down at him.

'You still don't understand, do you, Jason?'

With her blue eyes flashing and the heat of anger in her cheeks she was lovelier than ever. Jason had to force himself to remember that Morgan Muir was as conniving as the next woman. And more dangerous than most.

'I understand that you're no different from Vera.' His tone was cutting. 'Whatever you may have tried to prove, in the end you achieved the opposite.'

'Bastard!' Morgan hissed.

Jason laughed. 'I didn't say I didn't enjoy it.'

'Oh, but you're low.' Instinctively, Morgan's hand lifted and moved in the direction of his face.

'I wouldn't advise it,' Jason warned. 'Don't think for a moment that because you're a woman I won't retaliate if you hit me.'

With what looked to him like an effort, Morgan dropped her hand. Her chin was unnaturally high, her shoulders straight.

'You don't deserve affection,' she said jerkily.

'I don't need you to pass judgement on me, Morgan.'

But she pressed on, nevertheless. 'No wonder Vera left you. Any woman would find it hard to stay with a man who rejects tenderness and love.'

His dark eyes held her gaze. 'Love?' he asked in an odd tone.

She ignored the question. 'Any woman who tried to get close to you would be rejected.'

'Are you saying that *you* want to get close, Morgan?' Jason couldn't believe he had asked the question.

'Not on your sweet life!' she exclaimed. 'I'd be crazy to want to get close to you! Worse than crazy!'

'Is that so, Morgan?'

Jason leapt from his chair. As he closed the distance between them Morgan had no chance to escape. Once more his kisses were passionate, demanding a response from her—one which she seemed determined not to give. He felt as if he was staking a claim of some sort, and that made no sense at all.

He lifted his head when he became aware of small fists pummelling at his chest.

'You really are a bastard!' She threw the words at him. 'An absolute swine!'

'Aren't you being a bit dramatic?' he mocked.

'*Dramatic?* You condemn *me* for kissing *you*, and a moment later you launch into some primitive caveman attack! No wonder you don't have a woman in your life.'

Beneath his tan Jason was a little pale. 'Watch what you say, Morgan.'

'I refuse to take back a word of it!'

Her eyes shone with the glint of tears and those lovely kissable lips quivered. Jason hated to see a woman cry. Vera had cried whenever she was unable to get her way. At first her weeping had unnerved him, but after a while he had learned to harden himself against it.

Jason saw Morgan swallow, and then she was blinking the tears away. Something contracted in him at the sight.

'I take it you'll leave the ranch now,' he said as she made to leave the room.

Morgan did not answer immediately. Jason watched the slender shoulders straighten and the small head lift on the dainty neck. Slowly she turned back to him.

'I won't leave,' she said tightly. 'You should know that by now. You can be as mean as you like, Jason, but I will *not* let you ruin my dream for me.'

CHAPTER FOUR

MORGAN had her first riding lesson the next morning.

Jason was waiting for her when she returned to the ranch-house after cooking breakfast for the cowboys. Her eyes widened when she saw the riding gear he had laid out on the sofa in the living-room.

Jason grinned at her obvious surprise. 'Still have that dream, don't you?'

'Strong as ever.'

'And I told you that the only way to see a ranch properly was on horseback.'

The look she shot him was suspicious. Evidently Morgan had not expected this friendly Jason. If anything, she had probably been prepared for battle.

'I remember. But I thought...'

'That after calling me some choice names last night the offer was off?'

'Something like that.'

Jason's eyes sparkled. 'Seems I'm stuck with you—for a month.' For some reason he found it necessary to add the last words.

'That's right!'

'Get ready to ride, in that case. Good idea to make an early start before the worst of the heat.'

'These things...' She gestured. 'Do I need all this stuff?'

'The stetson will protect you from the sun.'

'That, yes. But the pants?'

Jason's deliberate glance at Morgan's posterior was tempered with a grin. 'I think you'll find they provide more padding than your jeans. They may be a bit big for you but you probably have a belt. As for the boots, with any luck they'll fit.'

'We'll see, won't we?' Morgan grinned back at him as she picked up Vera's gear and left the room.

Jason was getting the horses ready when Morgan walked into the stables. His hands stilled on a saddle as he watched her approach. How different Vera's clothes looked on Morgan—from the jaunty slant of the stetson to the pants, neatly belted but still a little loose on her slender figure.

Morgan had style, Jason thought unwillingly. There was more to it than that she was a model who had learned how to dress for the camera. Her classiness owed only a little to the way she wore her clothes. It was a quality that was evident in the way she was adapting to Brent's job, in her voice, her smile and her manner. Morgan's classiness was an integral part of the whole woman.

Her eyes were on the horses. 'I'm going to ride one of those?'

She looked so awed that Jason laughed. 'What did you think?'

'They're very big,' she said doubtfully.

'You said you'd been on a horse before.'

'Smaller than these two,' Morgan said. And then, see-ing the sparkle in the dark eyes, added reluctantly, 'OK, a lot smaller. More of a pony, if you must know.'

'The granddaughter of a cowboy on a pony! Borders on criminal. What would the old man have said if he'd known?'

'I'm sure you can guess.' Morgan laughed and, not for the first time, Jason thought the sound was like music on the silent air.

'Sure can,' he said drily. 'I'm still amazed that he didn't teach you to ride.'

Morgan's eyes clouded. 'I told you the reason.'

'And so now you look at these horses and think they're pretty big. Second thoughts, Morgan?'

'Not for a moment!'

'In that case, you may as well take Mayhem.' Jason gestured towards the smaller of the two horses, a gelding.

'Mayhem?' Again there was that lovely laugh. 'Intend to dispose of me so quickly?'

Jason laughed back at her. 'You'll be glad to know that Mayhem doesn't live up to his name. In fact, he's one of the gentlest horses on the ranch.'

'Do I have to take your word for that?'

'Absolutely.'

Their laughing eyes met and held, and Jason felt a swift stab of desire.

Then he was holding out a carrot and sugar and saying, 'Make friends, Morgan.'

Morgan hesitated as the horse's lips drew back to reveal teeth that looked as if they could quite easily clamp down on a human hand. She seemed about to take a step backwards. Then, as if she was thinking of her grandfather, she remained still as the horse took the food from her fingers. When all the food was gone she looked up at Jason.

'Cowboy's granddaughter,' he said with a grin.

Her eyes shone. 'That's exactly what I am.'

Jason took the reins of both horses and Morgan followed him into a corral outside the stables, where he gave her a few basic instructions.

'Most of this can't be new to you, Morgan,' he said when he had finished.

'You're right. I've spent years listening to my grandfather talk about his beloved horses.'

He shot her a wry look. 'Meaning I've bored you?'

'Oh, no, Jason, I wasn't bored!'

God, the way she was looking at him! The eagerness

in her eyes, the softly parted lips, the rise and fall of her breasts beneath the red blouse. Once more Jason felt that swift flaring of desire. Perhaps, after all, it had been a mistake to ride with her.

'Ready to mount?' he asked, his tone a trifle abrupt.

'Oh, yes!'

And then he was helping her up onto the horse, one hand cupping her arm and the other guiding a leg into the stirrups. He was not surprised at the intensified desire he felt when he touched her, the temptation to let his hand remain on her waist longer than was necessary. The thing was not to let himself give in to his emotions.

He looked up at her. 'OK?'

She shot him a sparkling smile. 'All ready to go.'

'Horse still seem big to you?'

'Enormous.'

'Frightened?'

'Why would I be? You'll be with me, won't you, Jason?'

He searched her face for signs of flirtatiousness or provocation, but didn't see any. There was just that glow in her eyes and a look of complete trust.

At that moment Jason knew that he would protect this girl with his life. At the same moment his sense of danger returned, and with it a dread feeling of inevitability that he did not like one bit. Morgan Muir was weaving some kind of magic around him, and he was damned if he knew what to do about it.

'Let's get going, then,' he said gruffly, and swung a leg over the back of his own horse.

Before long they were on a path leading through the brush. Where the trail was wide they rode side by side and where it narrowed the horses went in single file, with Jason's horse taking the lead.

Riding through the brushlands became a new experience for Jason as he made an effort to see the ranch through Morgan's eyes. As far as they could both see, north and south and east and west, there was brush— pasture for the thousands of cattle that grazed at Six-Gate Corral.

Once he stopped to let Morgan catch up with him. 'Well?' he asked.

'It's wonderful, Jason!'

'As your grandfather described it?'

'Almost exactly so. The sense of distance, of vastness and freedom. The great sky and the endless brush, the horizons that seem to extend to the ends of the earth and beyond.'

Her eagerness was infectious. After a moment, he said, 'You haven't seen much yet. You've barely scratched the surface.'

'I know.' She shot him an engaging smile. 'Which is precisely why I want to stay here a month.'

He had fallen into a trap of his own making, Jason thought wryly, but for some reason he couldn't be angry with Morgan or with himself.

'What are those cattle?' she asked, pointing in the distance.

He followed the line of a slim hand. 'Kashmirs.'

'That's what I thought.'

'You'd know about the various breeds, of course.'

She smiled again. 'Colour, shape, characteristics. Even the odd quirks and personality traits.'

'I'll bet,' Jason said with a laugh.

Morgan asked many questions and Jason found himself telling her about the different kinds of stock on the ranch, the problems he faced with drought and certain feed, the experiments he was busy with and the improvements he was hoping to make. Her questions were intelligent and thoughtful and when he replied she listened quietly, her expression interested.

For Jason, having been alone for so long—for in the

ways that counted he had been alone even when he had
been married to Vera—the fact that he could have so
much fun with a woman was a revelation. There was not
a moment when he was not aware of Morgan physically,
but now there was camaraderie, too, and a sense of joy
in her company.

He stiffened when he realized the drift of his thoughts.
In so many ways Morgan was different from Vera, yet
she was just as wrong for him as his ex-wife had been.
More so, in fact, because she could hurt him far more
deeply. He had only to look at Morgan—vibrant and
fragile—to know that she would never be happy living
indefinitely on a ranch. A month would be as much as
she could take. And when she went he would be lonelier
than ever because she was giving him a taste of what
his life could be like.

Jason was suddenly very angry. Angry with Morgan
for choosing Six-Gate Corral to pursue her dream. Angry
with himself for allowing her to affect him so intensely.
The trail was wide at this point, so wide that they could
easily go on riding side by side, but he dug his feet into
Thunder's flanks, leaving a bewildered Morgan to stare
at his rigid back.

So deep in thought was Jason that he didn't notice the
grove of trees, and by the time he did see them the trees
were all around them. Slowing Thunder, he looked back
at Morgan.

'Keep your head down!' he shouted.

Obediently she lowered her head, but not far enough.
A clump of low-hanging branches loomed threateningly,
spiky and dangerous. There was no time to call out further instructions.

Jason's decision was instantaneous. Wheeling
Thunder around, he closed in beside Mayhem, seized the
reins and at the· same time pushed down on Morgan's
head until it was flat on the head of her horse. With his

own head against Thunder's, he guided both horses through the trees.

As they emerged from the grove Jason heaved a sigh of relief. His hand left Morgan's head, but he didn't let go of Mayhem's reins.

'You can sit up,' he ordered gruffly.

She looked at him with a smile. 'Thanks for rescuing me. I would have been knocked off the horse if you hadn't acted so quickly.'

'I should have seen the trees,' he said, still in that same gruff tone.

'We came upon them so suddenly.'

'That's not an excuse. I know every inch of the ranch.' What he didn't tell Morgan was that it was only because he had been so busy thinking about her that he had not been concentrating on his surroundings.

Morgan's eyes shone, and that was incredible. Any another woman would have looked shaken, but she seemed exhilarated. As if she had actually enjoyed the experience.

Jason had been about to release Mayhem's reins but instead his grip on them tightened. As he leaned towards her Morgan's expression changed. Her small tongue flicked her lips, and her cheeks were suddenly flushed. She knew he wanted to kiss her. Once again anger came to Jason's rescue.

'I was at fault for getting us into the mess,' he growled, 'but how about you? Didn't you know enough to lie low on your horse? Good grief, Morgan, didn't your cowboy grandfather teach you anything of importance?'

'Maybe there were things he thought were best taught by someone else.' That was a provocative statement, if ever Jason had heard one.

For a moment he leaned even closer, so close that he could feel her breath warm against his face. His lips were just inches from hers; it would take no effort at all for them to meet. And then he remembered that for all her enthusiasm Morgan Muir would never be anything but a city girl—that this ride through the brush was just an experience to tell her friends about later and that she would be gone from here soon. At the last second he pulled back.

They looked at each other for a long moment while the air around them sizzled with electricity. Then, abruptly, Jason released Mayhem's reins and galloped ahead on Thunder.

They did not ride side by side again. Not another word passed between them until they were back at the stables.

Jason's face was sombre as he came out of the house, holding a dish. 'Scot,' he called.

The dog didn't respond, a fact which did not surprise Jason. He knew the place where Scot spent most of his time these days, and there he was, lying in the shade of a pine tree with his head resting on his paws. As Jason approached Scot's eyes opened, his ears lifted and his tail gave a cheerful if tired wag.

'Lunchtime, pal,' Jason said, putting the dish on the ground beside the dog.

Scot sniffed the air beside the dish, but didn't stir. That, too, didn't surprise Jason.

'Mince,' he said, 'with rice and gravy. Just the way you like it.'

Scooping a bit of the mixture onto his fingers, he held it against the dog's lips. Only now, and apparently only to please his master, did Scot put out his tongue.

Jason's expression was distressed as he began to feed the dog who was no longer much interested in food. Scot, his beloved pet, was growing old.

Jason had only to close his eyes to see in his mind the pup, runt of a litter of six, which he had decided to keep for himself. Weak as Scot had been at birth, he had quickly turned into a playful puppy—agile and so intelligent that Jason had known that he would be an excellent working dog. In this he had been proved correct. Scot was the best dog he had ever owned—loyal, brave and enormously affectionate.

Jason loved all dogs, but Scot had always been special. From the beginning he had had the run of the ranch-house, and in the last few years had slept by Jason's bed at night.

The fact that this much-beloved dog was growing older and frailer by the day was a source of great pain for Jason.

Dipping his fingers into the warm food which he himself had cooked, he held them once more to the dog's lips. Slowly, little by little, Scot was getting the nourishment he needed.

Jason didn't know when he suddenly realized that he was not alone. Turning his head, he saw Morgan nearby.

He lifted his head. 'Morgan… I didn't hear you.' He wondered how long she had been there, watching him.

'I'm sorry,' she said softly, 'I didn't mean to intrude.'

'Yes.' He didn't have to ask what she meant.

She moved closer. 'Is Scot ill?'

'He…isn't well.'

'I'm sorry. Can something be done?'

'Scot's real problem isn't illness, Morgan. He's just very old.'

'And you're doing all you can to help him.'

Jason saw the compassion in Morgan's face and looked away, but not before she had seen pain in his eyes.

'It isn't easy,' she said softly.

He was caught by something in her tone. 'You say that as if you know…'

'I do. I once had a cat that I loved. She was the most

playful kitten you can imagine. It never occurred to me when I watched her skimming up trees that she would ever grow old.'

'Do you still have her?'

'No.' Morgan was silent a moment. Then, still in that soft voice, she said, 'We love our pets so much and we get so attached to them. Seeing them like this and knowing that there's nothing we can do is incredibly hard.'

Jason didn't answer. He couldn't speak over the pain that filled his chest and rose up in his throat. He hoped that Morgan wouldn't ask him any more questions. He was in no mood for conversation. At this moment he just needed to be alone with his dog.

But Morgan didn't say another word. She just turned and walked away. Jason watched her for a moment—a slim figure, feminine, incredibly graceful. Then he bent once more to the dish, his lips tightening as he scooped a little more food onto his fingers.

Damn the woman! Whenever he thought he could harden himself against her she somehow managed to creep through his defences. That compassion of hers. He didn't want Morgan's understanding in a situation that was becoming more painful by the day. It was just as well she had walked away. If she had stayed he might actually have opened up to her—might have told her about his fears for his dog, about the sadness he tried so hard to suppress. And afterwards he would regret that he had confided in her.

'If I'm not careful I'll miss her when she goes,' Jason told the dog. 'She's so darn stubborn, always talking about that precious dream of hers, but there has to be some way of making her leave.'

There was only one thing to do.

'Round-up,' he said a few days later.

'Really?' The face that lifted to his was eager.

An eagerness that would vanish with the heat and the work. By the time the day ended little Miss Morgan Muir would be in quite a hurry to put distance between herself and Six-Gate Corral.

Hardening himself against the excited sparkle in the lovely blue eyes, Jason kept his own expression impersonal. 'Cowboy's granddaughter—guess I don't have to tell you what a round-up is.'

'Of course not! Round-ups were an integral part of my grandfather's lore. Cutting the calves from the herds and then branding them. I've been dying to see one, Jason.'

'Don't think it will be pretty.'

'I won't.'

'Not quite what you see in the movies.'

'A moment ago you called me the granddaughter of a cowboy, and now you're trying your best to put me off.' Her expression was saucy, her lips tilted in a way that made Jason want to kiss her.

He managed a shrug. 'Just telling you in advance what to expect. You may be repulsed by what happens.'

A mischievous grin. 'I'll take my chances.'

'Hot and dusty.'

She cocked her head at him cheekily. 'Seems to me this isn't the first time I've heard these doom-and-gloom warnings.'

Annoying female. 'And,' Jason said, 'if you think you're just coming along to watch you're mistaken— you'll be there to work.'

'Great!'

She wasn't reacting at all the way she was supposed to. 'Heavy work, Morgan. And not in the air-conditioned environs of the cookhouse.'

'In a chuckwagon?' she asked eagerly.

'That's right.'

'Wonderful!'

'Don't kid yourself, Morgan,' Jason said harshly. 'It won't be wonderful at all.'

'Why not?'

'Just telling you as it is. It will be blazing hot in the chuckwagon, hotter than even you can imagine. And you'll be running your feet off, preparing food for the cowboys.'

'You really are trying to put me off, Jason.'

'Round-up is tough work, Morgan. Just so long as you understand. The men will want to eat and drink.'

'Fine.' Incredibly she was still smiling. 'There've been no more complaints, have there? Not since that first time?'

'No,' Jason said shortly, reluctantly, after a moment. If anything, the men had been singing the praises of Morgan's cooking to him. A few, the starry-eyed Charlie in particular, would have been quite happy to have Morgan remain at Six-Gate Corral as their permanent cook.

'I'll manage this too,' she told him.

Was there no getting through to the girl? 'We'll see,' he said.

There was a part of Jason that felt guilty at the ordeal through which he was about to put Morgan. The chuckwagon was the time-honoured kitchen during round-up. It would be set up a little distance from the milling herds, and there the cook would work to keep the cowboys fed.

In recent years the practice had been discontinued at the ranch for Brent was getting too frail to toil under such difficult conditions.

Jason was fond of the old cowboy who had started work at Six-Gate Corral when Jason's father had been the rancher here. In those early days Brent had been known for his fearlessness and his daring, and although some things were too difficult for him now Jason had never had the heart to replace him and never would. Six-

Gate Corral would be Brent's home for as long as he wanted it. But a few changes had been made.

At round-up time Brent would prepare the food ahead in the air-conditioned cookhouse and the cowboys would carry it with them.

Morgan could have prepared the day's food in advance as well. But the chuckwagon would break her spirit as nothing else seemed to do.

Next morning Jason and Morgan left the stables together. It was the first time they had spent any length of time in each other's company since she had come upon him so unexpectedly when he'd been feeding Scot. Jason wondered if Morgan knew that he had been avoiding her deliberately. If she did, she hadn't commented on the fact.

Now and then, when his eyes went to the dainty figure on Mayhem's back, he realized how much he had been missing Morgan's company. The thought gave him no pleasure as he tried—without much success—not to let her closeness affect him. It was becoming more and more important to remember that she would leave Six-Gate Corral when the month ended—if not today when she had finished her duties in the chuckwagon.

The cowboys had been on the range since daybreak. By the time Morgan and Jason arrived at the scene of the round-up the chuckwagon had been set up and the cowboys were already hard at work, kerchiefs tied around their noses and mouths to keep out the swirling dust. Eagerly Morgan sat forward in her saddle and looked at the activity all around her.

'Guess you'd like to see a bit before you start your duties?' Jason said.

'Yes!'

It would be her only chance to see a round-up, Jason thought. That being the case, he was a willing guide, showing and explaining as much as he could of a scene which Morgan's grandfather had evidently described very often. A scene that was dramatic and thrilling and which had not changed very much since the days of the early western frontiers.

Morgan looked fascinated as she watched from a small hill near the chuckwagon. The range was a milling mass of cattle, horses and men. In and out the cowboys rode, swinging their lariats as they cut the calves from the herd. Strong men, tough and daring, as Morgan's grandfather had once been.

There was more to the round-up than just cutting and branding, and Jason showed Morgan everything. Some of it was not easy to witness, but Morgan was unflinching as she took it all in. Jason kept waiting for her to say that she'd had enough, but she didn't give him that satisfaction. She was keen to see everything.

'Have to get to work myself,' he said after a while. 'You'll be OK here alone?'

She smiled at him. 'Sure I will.'

'The men will be wanting to eat soon, Morgan.'

'I'm ready to start cooking any time now.'

Jason glanced at his watch. 'Half an hour longer, and I'll be back to take you to the chuckwagon.'

From her vantage point on the hill Morgan was glad to be watching the scene on her own because it gave her the chance to observe Jason at work.

Her eyes were only on him now, watching him dart in and out of the herd. A tall rugged figure, he was utterly at home on his horse and in this vast land. A man, Morgan thought, who would never ask anything of his men that he could not do just as well, if not better. Even from a distance he exuded a raw sexuality that was as much a part of him as his boots and his stetson.

Once a calf escaped from the herd and ran in the direction of the hill. Jason didn't wait for one of the cowboys to go after it but chased it himself, swinging his lariat as he rode. Deftly he roped the calf and swung it up towards him.

Morgan's heart was beating hard as she watched the man who was as vital as any of the cowboys. Fearless, powerful, more than a bit of a daredevil.

Insanely she found herself envying the calf that was now cradled in Jason's arms—that was where *she* wanted to be.

More than once in the last few days she had wondered whether what she felt for the tall rancher could possibly be love. Fervently she had hoped it was not that because it seemed obvious that her feelings were not returned. Just look how he had been avoiding her recently—a man in love would never do that.

Yet as she watched him now she could no longer hide the truth from herself: she was in love with Jason. Deeply, passionately, in love. She had not wanted to it to happen, not with a man who only wanted to see the back of her.

Morgan could have watched all day from her place on the hill, but after what seemed no time at all—it didn't seem possible that half an hour could have passed—Jason returned to her. Tanned arms rippled with hard muscle and dark eyes sparkled as he jumped from his horse.

Desire gripped her suddenly, powerful and over-whelming—a longing to reach up and nuzzle her lips against Jason's throat, to shape her fingers around the contours of his body, to explore him. A primordial desire, raw and fierce and throbbing, so all-pervading that Morgan trembled. Nobody before Jason had ever succeeded in evoking this kind of feeling in her. Instinct told her that she would never feel this way with any man again.

Wordlessly she looked back. Then she swallowed

hard and prodded Mayhem into motion: it was time for her to get to work.

Jason had not exaggerated. Inside the chuckwagon it was hot. So hot that for a few moments Morgan felt dizzy. But she was determined not to let the heat get the better of her. When she had splashed her face, neck and wrists with cool water she began the meal preparations. Soon the cowboys would start arriving for their food, and she had to be ready for them.

Come they did. She gave them big bowls of chili, huge steaks and bread she had baked in advance in the cookhouse. She provided cool drinks as well as mugs of tea, sweetened with sugar.

Charlie came. He praised the food and was eager to stand around and talk, drinking his tea slowly to make it last as long as he could.

Hank came too. As always, Morgan was on her guard with the man. She answered him when he spoke—coolly dismissive when his comments were offensive and aloof when the insolent gaze ravished her face and body in that blatant way that he had. Morgan had taken Hank's measure: she wouldn't let him get the better of her.

And then Jason appeared at the chuckwagon, and Morgan's breath caught in her throat. He was so big, so powerful, dominating the small space with his presence. Sexy at the best of times, now—with his cowboy clothes dampened by sweat—he was irresistible. She took a step towards him, then made herself move back. He would think her crazy if she gave in to the impulse to push the strands of damp hair from his forehead.

For a minute at least he stood looking down at her, his hands squarely on his hips as his gaze raked her face before descending to her body. She saw one expression give way to another, and wished she knew what he was thinking. When he looked up at her face once more his eyes were sombre.

'Ready for something to eat?' she asked, her tone deliberately light in order to break the odd tension.

'Eat?' For a moment he looked surprised, as if food had not been on his mind. Then he shrugged. 'Sure, why not?'

She watched him take a few spoonfuls of chili. 'Well?' she asked when he looked at her again.

'It's good.'

'That's it?' The tension had lessened by now and she was able to laugh. 'Charlie said it was the best chili he'd ever eaten. And even Hank said—among a few other things—that it wasn't bad.'

Jason's face darkened. 'Hank had been here already. Did he come again?'

'Yes.'

'What did he say?'

'Nothing of consequence.'

'Why don't I believe you?' he asked.

There was an expression on his face which made Morgan think of a man getting ready to punch another man in the jaw.

'I've no idea why you don't believe me,' she said lightly. And then she went on, 'No point in talking about Hank, is there? Only gives the guy power he doesn't deserve. You can't do anything about him anyway, Jason.'

Except to fire the man, she thought. Instinctively she knew that the same thought was going through Jason's mind.

'You don't want to do that,' she said. She laughed again as his head jerked. 'No, Jason, I'm not a mind-reader, but your face can be expressive—when you're not being deliberately poker-faced—and just now it was grim. How *was* the chili, anyway?'

'Deft change of subject.' Jason's expression lightened as he grinned. 'OK, we won't talk about Hank, we'll talk about the chili instead. It's delicious, just as Charlie said.'

'Gee, thanks,' she said saucily.

'Exhausted, Morgan?'

'Not at all,' she told him cheerfully.

'The heat must be too much for you.'

'Is it hot? Can't say I noticed.'

'You are lying, Morgan Muir.'

'Well, maybe just a little,' she teased.

'More than a little,' he insisted.

Her eyes sparkled. 'You are doing your darnedest to put words in my mouth, Jason Delaney, but it won't work.'

'Don't know what you're trying to say,' he countered abruptly.

'Oh, I think you do, Boss. Today was a test.'

'A test?' he repeated blandly.

'Admit it.'

'Why would I test you, Morgan?'

'You're trying your best to frighten me into leaving. It won't work, Jason.'

'Really?'

'No. I like it here, and I mean to stay.'

'I see.'

She grinned at him. 'You're disappointed.'

'Disappointed?'

'Don't pretend you're not. For reasons of your own you don't want me here. But I've passed the test, Jason. I've given you no reason to get rid of me. And I'm not about to leave on my own.'

In the rugged face an unreadable expression came and went. 'Don't tell me you've actually enjoyed the experience,' he said disbelievingly.

'But I have. Every minute of it.' She was laughing again.

'This was only one day,' Jason said harshly. 'If you

told me you'd enjoy doing this in the long term I wouldn't believe you.'

Something tightened inside Morgan at his words, but she tried not to show it. As lightly as she could she said, 'Who's talking long-term?'

She held her a breath a moment, but when he didn't answer she went on, still in the same light tone, 'I came here for a month, Jason, to experience the life my grandfather lived. I didn't imagine it would be cool or air-conditioned or that I'd be sleeping late every morning. And if you think I'm complaining, I'm not. *This* is the way I'd imagined it. Just like this, Jason. I wouldn't want it to be any different.' And then, to prove that she expected nothing of him, she added, 'None of which means I've ever thought of my stay as long-term.'

Jason's eyes darkened ominously, his lips suddenly tight.

After a moment Morgan said, a little uncertainly this time, 'You really are disappointed, aren't you? That I passed the test?'

'You flatter yourself if you think that.' Jason's tone was so inexplicably harsh that Morgan almost felt as if he had hit her.

Her blue eyes were suddenly confused. What on earth did Jason think she had said? 'I only meant...' She stopped.

'What *did* you mean, Morgan?'

'You thought I'd fail the test, and I didn't. I'll work in the chuckwagon again tomorrow.'

The rugged-featured face was tight. 'No,' Jason said.

'Why not? Are you going to tell me I didn't do the job properly?'

'You did OK,' he admitted grudgingly.

'Well, then?'

His lips still tight, he looked at her. He seemed about to speak and then apparently thought better of it.

'What is it, Jason? Please tell me.'

'There's nothing to say.'

'But there is. This morning you were all gung-ho about me working in the chuckwagon. Part of the job, you said.'

'True…'

'What's happened since then, Jason? Why have you changed your mind?'

'It doesn't matter,' he said curtly.

'It does to me,' Morgan cried.

'It doesn't matter,' Jason said again.

And then it came to Morgan. 'You really *were* trying to scare me into leaving. That's what today was all about.'

Inside Morgan a knife of pain tore at her chest. Why did Jason dislike her so much?

'It didn't work,' she said dully.

'No?'

'No, Jason, I'm staying.'

'That's up to you.'

'And I want to work in the chuckwagon again.'

'I've already said no to that.'

'Are you going to tell me why not?'

Jason hesitated a second. 'No,' he said.

'Jason—'

'I said no.' His tone defied further argument.

CHAPTER FIVE

A WEEK after Morgan had worked in the chuckwagon she went once more to the stables. Only this time she went alone.

Ben, the young cowboy who tended Jason's personal horses, looked distinctly uneasy when he heard her request.

'The ranch is a big place, Morgan. Thousands of acres of brush. Person can lose their way and never be found. And then there's the mesquite—bad stuff that.'

'I know all about the mesquite,' Morgan tried to reassure him, 'and I won't get lost.' Seeing Ben's doubtful look, she added, 'I just want to ride out to the round-up. I've been there with Jason. I know where it is.'

Conflicting expressions came and went in the young cowboy's face. He was obviously having a hard time deciding what to do. 'Don't know if Jason will like it,' he said at last. 'Maybe I should go with you.'

'I'd really like to go alone, Ben. I don't think there'll be a problem with Jason, but if there is, I'll take the blame, I promise.'

Ten minutes later Morgan was on Mayhem's back and riding away from the stables. A worried-looking Ben watched her go, and she threw him a cheerful wave.

Though a week had gone by since she had been to the round-up with Jason, Morgan had no trouble finding the way. There was a trail she remembered, landmarks she recognized. Even the grove of trees posed no problems for she was looking out for them.

She didn't mind riding alone—if anything, she enjoyed it. Granddaughter of a cowboy, she felt utterly at home on Mayhem's back in the vast ranch-lands. Even the heat didn't bother her as much as it had at the start.

About an hour after leaving the stables Morgan came to the round-up. She smelled and heard it long before she actually reached it. There were the shouts of the cowboys, the snorting of animals and the clouds of dust kicked up by frantic hooves.

On the hill where, a week earlier, she had watched with Jason she reined Mayhem in. Once again the scene her grandfather had described to her so often came alive before her eyes. Cowboys on horseback, heading the calves away from their mothers before roping them. Other cowboys tending to the branding, applying the distinctive Six-Gate Corral mark which Jason had shown her the first time. The throbbing vitality, the sense of danger, the toil.

The best view was from a rock-pile at the edge of the hill. Dismounting, Morgan tethered Mayhem to a small tree that had been bent almost double by years of wind. Then she made her way alone onto the rocks.

Jason didn't notice the girl and the horse. As before, he worked with the cowboys—a superb figure on a powerful horse, weaving in and out of the herd. It was Charlie who saw her first, his eyes caught by the flash of red blouse on the hill. 'Hey, there's Morgan!' she heard him call.

Some of the other cowboys were looking towards the hill now but not Jason because he was riding at some distance from Charlie and the others. Hank shouted something. Morgan couldn't make out the words but from his jeering expression and Charlie's angry stance she could guess at a ribaldry of some sort. Work forgotten, more cowboys were also looking her way now.

Jason must have sensed that something was happening for he lifted his head. He stared at Morgan a few seconds, as if he couldn't believe what he was seeing. Then he pulled in his lariat and rode towards the hill.

Gladly Morgan scrambled over the rocks to meet him. It was only when he dismounted that she saw his unsmiling face and the rigidity of his stance.

'What do you think you're doing here?' he demanded.

'Jason—' Morgan began uncertainly.

'You should be at the ranch,' Jason said furiously, without letting her speak.

'I came to see the round-up,'

'You've seen it already.'

'Only once.'

'Once is enough.'

'No, Jason, not really. I spent most of that day in the chuckwagon. I didn't watch for long. I wanted to see it again.'

'You had no right, Morgan.'

She stared at him. 'Right?' she echoed.

'You should have asked me if it was OK for you to come.' Jason's expression was hard.

'*Asked*?' Morgan's voice had turned mutinous.

'You heard me.'

'I think that what you mean,' she corrected him carefully, through the stirrings of her own anger, 'is that I should have *mentioned* it. I would have, Jason, but you were gone by the time I thought of it.'

'You should have stayed at the house in that case.'

'Doing what?' Morgan's tone was dangerously light.

'Things women do,' Jason said aloofly.

'And those are?'

'You know the answer better than I do, Morgan. I shouldn't have to tell you.'

'Cooking? Cleaning?' Any pretence at lightness vanished as she flung the words at him furiously. 'I'd done all that. Prepared breakfast for the men, made their lunches and packed them. Cooked your breakfast.

Cleaned the house. Yes, I know that house-cleaning isn't part of my duties but I've been doing it all the same.'

'What are you getting at?' Jason asked tensely.

'I'd done everything I could think of, and I was bored. Bored right out of my mind. Can you understand that, Jason?'

Jason's eyes were suddenly bleak. 'Oh, yes, I understand.'

'You do?' It wasn't the answer she had expected.

'Vera was bored too. That was one of the problems with our marriage. Vera was bored with the ranch. So bored that she began to distance herself from it all soon after the honeymoon. If you're bored, Morgan, you shouldn't have come here in the first place.'

'You've told me so a million times,' she flared at him. 'I'm sick and tired of hearing it.'

He gave an autocratic shrug. 'I won't waste my time saying it again, in that case.'

Hurt by his cool, implacable tone, Morgan gave a short, unamused laugh. 'You dislike me so much.'

His dark eyes were shuttered all at once, making them impossible to read. 'Dislike,' Jason said distantly, 'has nothing to do with my feelings at this moment. You shouldn't have come to the round-up, Morgan, and I'm quite sure you know that. To get back to what I said before, you had no right to come here without asking me first.'

Morgan's head jerked. 'I'm not a child, Jason. I don't have to ask your permission for the things I do.'

'I happen to be your employer and the owner of this ranch,' he reminded her tautly.

'You're also a chauvinist.' Outraged, she tossed the words at him.

'A chauvinist?' he exploded.

'Don't tell me that's news to you. Or that you don't know what the word means.'

'I know precisely what it means,' Jason drawled. 'It's an insult. One Vera used whenever she couldn't get her own way.' He paused for a moment. 'A chauvinist—is that how you see me, Morgan?'

Her eyes flashing with spirit, Morgan said, 'What should I think when you seem to believe I ought to spend all my time doing so-called "womanly" things. Activities that you sanction. I like cooking for the men, Jason, but that wasn't my reason for coming to the ranch.'

'May I remind you—' Jason was calmer now, and all the more dangerous for it '—that it was at my suggestion that you went out on Mayhem in the first place. That I taught you to ride.'

'I don't deny it for a moment. What are you leading up to, Jason? Haven't I shown you enough gratitude?'

He took a quick step forward and his hand shot out to grip her chin, holding it in fingers that bit tightly into her soft skin. 'I've never expected gratitude from you, Morgan.'

Standing just inches away from him, Morgan was acutely aware of his maleness, his vitality. She had a wild impulse to throw herself into his arms, to kiss the anger from his eyes and the hardness from his lips—to tell him how much she hated the things they were saying. But she needed to focus on his words, to concentrate on her own responses.

'What are you getting at, then, Jason?'

'I didn't expect you to take advantage.'

She twisted away from his hand, trying to ignore the burning sensation on her skin where his fingers had been. '*Advantage*?'

'What do you call it, Morgan? Riding off alone the moment my back was turned. You must have known how I'd feel about it.'

For the first time since she'd left the stables Morgan remembered the young cowboy. Ben had tried to warn her that Jason would not take easily to her going out alone on Mayhem.

'Did you think I wouldn't manage?' she asked uneasily.

'You've shown that you can cope with things.' Giving Morgan no time to enjoy the compliment, Jason went on, 'Fact is, you're a woman. Young. Pretty.'

'Jason...?' She looked up at him, her expression questioning.

'Don't make anything of what I just said.' The hard-boned features gave nothing away. 'I'm just trying to tell you that your appearance makes you vulnerable. And I'm not only talking about Hank. There's no way of knowing who could be roaming around in the brush.'

'I can take care of myself, Jason.'

'Seems to me I've heard that before—something about self-defence skills.' His eyes sparkled as her cheeks grew red.

'I *can* defend myself, Jason. I will if I have to.'

'I hope you'll be successful.' His tone implied that he didn't believe her. The sparkle vanished as he went on grimly, 'Men aren't the only danger, Morgan. You learned to ride very quickly, but you're still inexperienced.'

'And you're going to tell me of all the terrible things that can happen to me. I could be kidnapped by cattle thieves or get slashed by the mesquite. Failing that, I could always be overcome by the heat.' She tilted her chin at him. 'Have I come up with all the dangers or are there any more you'd like to throw my way?'

Laughter glimmered unexpectedly in his dark eyes, and just for a second his sensuous lips tilted at the corners. 'Provocative girl but you know that, don't you?' Then Jason's expression hardened once more. 'Have you any idea how big this ranch is? Scoff all you like, Morgan, but you could have got lost.'

'No, because I knew where I was going. I'd been out this way with you.'

'A week ago.'

'I got here without any mishaps.'

Jason pushed back his stetson in a gesture of exasperation. 'How do I get through to you, woman? The brush is deceptive. You found your way today, but you can get lost more easily than you realize.'

'Anything else you want to tell me?'

'Yes, I'm ordering you not to ride alone again,' he said flatly.

'And if I do?' Morgan asked recklessly.

'Then you're out. Off this ranch. No matter when Brent gets back. No questions asked.'

Morgan could see that he meant it. If she took Mayhem out alone again Jason would not hesitate to fire her. And she wouldn't be able to do anything about it.

They stared at each other for several seconds, blue eyes meeting brown ones—clashing, holding. Then Jason said, 'By the way, did *you* saddle Mayhem?'

Morgan opened her mouth, only to close it again. It was bad enough that she was in trouble. She couldn't cause problems for Ben as well.

'You're not answering me, Morgan.'

'I…' She shifted her gaze.

'Ben was there, wasn't he? You got him to saddle the horse for you.'

'He didn't want to,' Morgan said quickly. 'He warned me that you wouldn't like it.'

'I'm sure he did.'

'Don't blame Ben,' Morgan pleaded. 'He didn't want me to go. I told him that if you were angry I'd take the blame.'

'So, then, you did know what you were doing.' The expression in the rugged face was intimidating.

'If you put it that way… But I didn't think there was

any harm in it, truly I didn't. Is Ben going to be in trouble, Jason? That wouldn't be fair.'

'It wouldn't,' Jason agreed. 'Particularly as I know only too well the effect you have on men. On Charlie, on Hank. And on—' He stopped abruptly.

'On…?' Morgan breathed.

But Jason refused to be drawn. 'Ben won't get into trouble, though he will get a warning—not to let a pair of blue eyes and a winsome smile get the better of his judgement.' And, before Morgan could take any sort of pleasure in the words, he added, 'It's time Ben learned that a woman's wiles can be the undoing of even the strongest man.'

Morgan flinched at his words. The rugged face was implacable, and hard eyes raked her face. Not for the first time, she wondered why Jason disliked her so much.

'Wiles,' she said dully. 'Does that mean you think I'm manipulative?'

'Aren't you?' Jason taunted.

'No!'

'You've done nothing but manipulate since you came here, Morgan.'

'No, Jason! That's not true.'

'Want some examples?' he asked evenly. 'They're not hard to find. You made sure of staying on the ranch when you weren't welcome. Today you persuaded a callow young cowboy to saddle a horse when you both knew that what he was doing was wrong. So, yes, Morgan, I see you as manipulative. Just like the rest of your gender.'

'You're comparing me with your ex-wife.' She flung the words at him without thinking.

'Leave Vera out of this.' Jason's voice was harsh.

Morgan felt a little ill. She hated the words she and Jason were bandying back and forth—the ugliness, the anger and the resentment. She had to look away from him so that he wouldn't see the tears that threatened to fill her eyes. She couldn't let him see her cry.

Only when she felt that she had the tears under control did she turn back to him. 'What about my dream?' she asked in a low voice.

'That again,' he said dismissively.

'Jason, you yourself said that the only way to see a ranch is on horse-back.'

'Not alone.'

'Does that mean I must always ask one of the men to accompany me?'

For some reason the question had Jason clenching his hands into fists. 'If you ride you ride with me.' Had Morgan not known better, something in his expression might have had her thinking that he was jealous.

'That's silly, Jason. If one of the others—Charlie, for instance—wanted to ride with me, that would be OK, surely?'

'If you ride you ride with me. Nobody else. Is that understood, Morgan?'

'You're worried that I might corrupt some poor trusting guy.' She knew that the statement was provocative.

'Let's just say that I'm not prepared to take the chance. You'll ride with me or not at all.'

'You're always busy, Jason.'

'Tough.' He was unsympathetic. 'Six-Gate Corral is a working ranch. You can come with me when I have the time but you will not take Mayhem out alone.'

'But, Jason—'

'Take it or leave it, Morgan. I'm not prepared to discuss it any further. I've already wasted enough time as it is.'

With those words, he wheeled his horse and rode away from her down the hill.

Minutes later he was back in the thick of all the frenzied activity, roping a steer with all the fearlessness of

a professional cowboy. Morgan climbed to a higher rock,
giving herself a better vantage point from which she
could watch the scene below. If Jason made it impossible
for her to ride then this could well be the last round-up
she witnessed.

She tried to commit to memory the scene before her,
one that was as old as Texas itself—the range, the cattle,
the horses. The cowboys, seemingly over their surprise
at seeing her, had gone back to their work. Morgan
watched as Hank skillfully roped a wayward calf. The
man might have some abhorrent personality defects, but
as a cowboy he was clearly hard to fault.

Half an hour or more had passed when a sudden
panic-stricken whinnying had her jerking around, just in
time to see her horse yanking itself loose from the tree
to which it had been tethered.

'Mayhem! Whoa! Stop!' Morgan shouted.

As quickly as she could she scrambled from rock to
rock, but was too late to stop the bolting horse. By the
time she reached the bottom of the rock-pile Mayhem
was already at the foot of the hill, galloping at breakneck
speed away from the round-up.

Wide-eyed, Morgan stared after the horse. What on
earth could have happened to spook it?

She froze at an ominous rattling sound. Without moving her feet, she turned her head. *A snake*! Not far from
the tree where Mayhem had been tethered. A rattlesnake.
Its body had small diamond markings and its tail was
raised.

In seconds the blood turned to ice in Morgan's veins.
Keep calm, she told herself as she took a shuddering
breath.

Minutes later, when she was still wondering how to
navigate her way safely around the snake, a horse and
rider came galloping up the hill.

'Saw Mayhem take off as if the devil was behind

him,' Jason shouted as he came into earshot. 'Thought you were on Mayhem's back!'

As he came closer Morgan saw that his face was pale despite the heat.

'Pictured you clinging to a horse that was out of control, Morgan. Caught by a low-hanging branch or falling in the mesquite. *Idiot woman*! You should never have come to the round-up. You're nothing but trouble.'

'Jason—'

Ignoring the desperate plea, Jason rushed on, 'Then I realized that you were still up here. What happened? Why did Mayhem bolt?'

Morgan could only point. Jason saw the snake immediately. In an instant he bent low, scooped Morgan up into his arms and placed her in front of him on the saddle.

'Keep still—and quiet.' He whispered the warning against her ear.

Not very far from the pawing horse the snake lifted its head. Tensely Morgan watched the striking movement she had seen only in movies. If Jason hadn't arrived when he had, what would have happened to her? As the full extent of the danger she'd been exposed to made its impact she began to shiver violently.

At the bottom of the hill Jason reined in his horse. Turning her head, Morgan looked at him. As their eyes met she saw something in the dark depths that she had never seen before—naked and hungry, deep and unguarded. Morgan recognized passion when she saw it— profound passion in a man whose emotions were normally kept under such iron control.

Her gasp was involuntary. She didn't know that her own eyes glazed over, that her lips parted. That she looked like a woman who wanted to be made love to.

Jason's hissing exhalation of breath was hot on her cheek. The muscles in the arms around her tightened.

They sat on the motionless horse, their eyes locked together and their hearts racing in unison, tense and still in a moment that was suspended in time. Now that the worst of the shock was over Morgan was overwhelmed by the urge to stay in Jason's arms for ever.

And then he was swinging his legs off the horse. 'Stay here,' Jason said crisply as he lifted Morgan to the ground, depositing her on a large sandy spot where movement of any kind would be easy to see. 'I'll be right back.'

'Jason—'

'Don't move. That's an order. One which even you had better heed, Morgan.' A wicked grin lit up his face. 'Unless, of course, you see another rattlesnake, in which case you move quickly.'

And then he was vaulting on the horse's back once more and riding in the direction of the cattle, the horses and the men.

Still shaken, Morgan did as Jason had asked and stayed where she was. By the time he returned, minutes later, her heart had slowed somewhat but it was still beating too fast.

He reined in his horse and once more their eyes met, but this time an enigmatic expression hid any emotion he felt. There was only a muscle flicking at the top of his throat and a pulse beating strongly at its base, but Morgan could make nothing of that.

Jason was the first to break the silence. 'I'm taking you back to the ranch-house, Morgan. I've just been to tell the men.'

'No, Jason!' she burst out. And, in a milder tone, went on, 'I understand how you feel about my riding alone— I won't do it again—but, now that I'm here, can't I stay?'

'Afraid not.'

'Why not?'

'It isn't a good idea.'

His words were firmly spoken, his manner unyielding. There it was again, the chauvinist streak she had complained of earlier. Morgan's heart sank. It was one thing to be in love with the man and quite another to know that she had to stand up to him.

Her chin went up. 'I didn't ride all this way to go back now.'

His expression was impatient. 'You're wasting my time, Morgan. I suppose you realize that? Time wasted, rescuing you from the rattlesnake. Time wasted, taking you to the house. Time that would be far better spent helping the men with the work.'

'You're so angry, Jason, and I'm sorry about the snake,' she said quietly, 'but I'd really like to stay and watch the round-up.'

His tone was implacable. 'My mind is made up.'

'So is mine.'

'You have no choice, Morgan. This is one thing that's not up for debate.'

Still she tried. 'Why do I have to go back? One good reason, Jason. And don't tell me about the heat and the dust, you know they don't worry me.' And as he stared at her aloofly, 'Give me one reason, Jason, just one.'

'It's dangerous,' he said flatly.

'With all this activity, I'll bet there aren't any more rattlesnakes around.'

'You never know when the cattle can veer in your direction. You don't want to be caught in a stampede.'

'The men seem to be controlling the herd really well, and I'm swift on my feet when I need to be. If you have a good reason, Jason, you haven't given it to me.'

His lips tightened ominously and his eyes were hard. 'The men,' he said after a moment.

This was the real reason, Morgan knew. 'I promise not to distract them,' she said slowly.

'A promise you could never keep.' Jason's voice was dry. 'You've been distracting them ever since you came to this ranch, Morgan Muir, and well you know it.'

'Not on purpose, Jason. Never once on purpose.'

'Maybe not, but it's been happening all the same. There's a different atmosphere in the bunkhouse these days. In the cookhouse. Cowboys who never gave a darn about their appearance before you arrived are now slicking down their hair before they come in for a meal.'

'Heavens!' Blue eyes sparkled mischievously. 'I had no idea. I thought they always freshened up after a day on the range.'

'Not necessarily.'

Morgan smiled at Jason. 'I'd have thought you'd be pleased that the men are taking some pride in themselves.'

'Pride isn't what it's all about, Morgan. It's the whiff of sex.'

'*Sex!*' she exclaimed.

'Sure. The cowboys, most of them, know they don't stand a chance with you, but that doesn't stop them trying to impress you. Ever since you came, Morgan, the cookhouse has turned into a yard of preening roosters, all of them vying for the attention of the solitary hen.'

Morgan burst out laughing. 'I've been called a few odd things in my life, but never a hen,' she said merrily. 'I believe you're making too much of this, Jason. If the men want to spruce up a bit before they eat, surely that isn't a big deal?'

'It is when it leads to tension,' Jason said grimly. 'Before you arrived on the scene, Morgan, the weekly Saturday evening foray into town was about the only time most of the guys had any contact with women. We're talking about hard outdoors men, cowboys who are usually content with a few beers in a bar and some dancing in the local saloon. Maybe more than that, but none of it very serious.'

'I'm not sure what you're trying to tell me, Jason.'

'Your presence at the ranch has changed everything.'

She looked at him thoughtfully. 'You speak as if there's never been a woman here before. Brent mentioned an Emily.'

'Emily was never a problem.'

'How about Vera? Didn't she cause a stir?'

'Vera didn't go near the men.'

'Because she was the boss's wife?'

'That was only part of it.'

'Part…?'

'Vera looked down her nose at the cowboys. She was always at me to seek out the company of what she called "more civilized people."'

'A snob, in other words.'

'Let's just say that Vera didn't care for the cowboys,' Jason said evenly.

Morgan looked at Jason, wondering about the woman he had married and wondering how much he still missed her. Wondering how he had come to marry someone who was so different from him in all the things that mattered. But she couldn't ask him the things she wanted so much to know—at least not at this moment.

'Vera's loss,' she said crisply, 'because, with one exception, the cowboys are a great bunch of guys.' She was quiet for a moment, before adding, 'Do you really think I'd distract them if I stayed to watch?'

'Roping and branding are dangerous. The men can't afford to have their concentration disturbed. Even a momentary lapse can be enough to cause a fatal mistake.'

'That's the only reason?' Morgan asked, sensing that there was something he wasn't telling her.

'The snake,' Jason said after a moment.

'It's on the hill, far from here.'

'Where there's one snake there can be others.'

Morgan shuddered. 'OK, I'll go back.' And then, curious because she didn't see a vehicle, she said, 'We're going by car?'

'On horseback.'

'I don't understand. I mean, with Mayhem gone...'

'You'll ride on my horse, Morgan.' And when she looked startled he added, '*With* me.'

Morgan's heart began a sudden wild beating, so loud that she imagined Jason could hear it over the noise of the cattle and the horses and the men.

'Behind me this time,' he told her drily.

Morgan was red-cheeked and silent as Jason lifted her onto the high saddle. Did his hands linger a moment longer than necessary on her waist, or was that just a product of her fevered imagination?

'Hold tight,' he said, and she did just that.

As the big horse galloped through the brush Morgan wrapped her arms around Jason's waist, a hold that grew progressively tighter as she thrilled to the ride. Everything thrilled her. The horse beneath her, a much bigger horse than Mayhem—powerful as the horses of legend. The countryside, hard and rugged and yet beautiful too. And the man.

More than anything else, there was the man. As rugged as the countryside that was his territory, and as beautiful. A sheerly masculine kind of beauty, all toughness and power and strength. And always, as if it was an integral part of him, there was the raw sexiness that seemed to override everything else.

Laying her cheek against his back, she closed her eyes—the better to experience sensations she would never forget.

Ride away with me, cowboy; ride, she told him silently. Keep riding. Into the sunset, into another day and the next. Don't let this ride end.

When the horse slowed from a gallop to a canter and finally to a walk Morgan opened her eyes. They were in the corral, approaching the stables. She hadn't even realized that they were so close to the house.

And there was Mayhem, already unsaddled. Morgan was relieved to see her horse. She had been worrying whether he would make it back to the stables alone.

Lifting her face from Jason's back, she loosened her grip around his waist. She was sitting upright by the time Jason leaped from the horse. He stood, looking up at her, one hand on his hip and the other holding the reins. For a long moment his expression was so enigmatic that it was impossible to guess at his thoughts. The enigmatic look vanished suddenly as his eyes took on a sparkle and his lips tilted in a grin.

Until that moment Morgan had persuaded herself that Jason hadn't realized quite how tightly she had been holding him—that he had been unaware of her face against his back. The wickedness of his grin told her that he had known all the time.

In a second heat flooded Morgan's cheeks. Shy all at once, she could not meet his gaze.

'Well, Morgan?' he asked softly.

Restlessly she shifted on the saddle. 'Yes?'

'Enjoy the ride?'

'It was OK,' she managed over the dryness in her throat.

Jason laughed, the low vibrant laugh that was as sexy as the rest of him. 'Now why did I think it was more than that? A lot more than just OK?'

A quiver shot through Morgan, as much at Jason's tone as at his words. She doubted whether his question needed an answer. She couldn't have given one in any case.

She was about to swing her own legs off the horse when Jason reached up and lifted her out of the saddle.

To Morgan's amazement he didn't put her down immediately but continued to hold her, his hands around her waist—her feet six inches or more above the ground. Light as she was, only a strong man could have held her thus for more than a few seconds. Jason didn't seem to be exerting any effort at all.

'I enjoyed it too,' he said, his mouth so close to hers that his breath was warm on her lips.

The way he was holding her she could feel the long length of him against her, warm and throbbing against her own pulsating body.

'Don't go riding alone again, Morgan.'

'No.' The word emerged jerkily.

'Imagine if the snake had got to you—if you'd been harmed, with no one about to help you.'

At the mention of the snake she shuddered again. '*Don't*! Jason... Jason, put me down.'

As if he hadn't heard her he held her even closer. 'Do you know what that would have done to me, Morgan?'

What? What would it have done to him?

'Caused you a bit of inconvenience?' she managed lightly. 'If the snake had got to me there'd have been things for you to do, things that would have taken you away from the round-up.'

'You have all the answers, don't you?' His voice was laced with a curious mixture of brusqueness and sarcasm.

'Put me down, Jason...'

'In a moment,' he said harshly.

One arm went around her back and with the other hand he tilted her head. Morgan tried to twist away, but with her feet above the ground she was as helpless as a rag doll in Jason's hands.

Slowly he began to taste her mouth, his lips touching hers so lightly that the contact was a kind of teasing torture with a maddened Morgan just barely able to restrain herself from screaming for more.

'Put me down,' she pleaded against his mouth. But Jason only laughed, a wild and reckless laugh, and then he was kissing her again. More tantalizing kisses, kisses that turned Morgan's body to fire and filled her with an aching tortuous hunger—a hunger so intense that she began to tremble quite violently.

Later Morgan could not have said how long their kisses had lasted. She knew only that she had never been quite so excited. That all she wanted was to rush into the house with Jason, to tear off his clothes and her own, and to make love.

But Jason, it seemed, had other ideas. Without warning he lifted his lips from hers and let Morgan's feet drop to the ground. Seconds later he had leaped on the horse and was riding back the way they had just come.

Morgan put a trembling finger to her burning lips. Why had Jason ended the embrace just as her own desire was mounting to the point where she could have denied him nothing? Was it possible that he hadn't known how she felt?

Feeling numb and a little dazed, she watched horse and rider vanish in the brush. Then she turned away and walked toward the ranch-house.

CHAPTER SIX

THEY were halfway through breakfast when Jason answered the phone.

'I want to speak to you, Jason. I *have* to speak to you.' The all-too-familiar whining tone belonging to Vera put him instantly on edge.

'Not now,' he said abruptly.

'Jason, *please*. There are things we need to talk about, and—'

'There isn't any point.'

Jason knew why Vera was calling. She had called him several times in the last weeks, always for the same purpose. During the course of their short marriage he had become so accustomed to her tone that it had ceased to bother him after a while. Perhaps because he had got used to a different kind of voice lately—one that was low and sweet and attractively modulated—Vera's whine irritated him now.

Without thinking, he looked at Morgan. Catching his eye, she stood up. She was about to go to the door when he called her back.

'Morgan…' It didn't occur to him to put his hand over the mouthpiece so that Vera, at the other end of the line, wouldn't hear him.

'Morgan?' Vera asked. 'You have a new man at the ranch?'

Morgan looked enquiringly at Jason. 'Sounds private. I don't want to intrude.'

Her voice must have carried through the line. 'Morgan is a *woman*?' Vera said angrily. 'You have a *woman* with you?'

111

Jason motioned to Morgan to stay. The meal she had prepared was delicious—sausages, grilled to perfection, and a fluffy cheese omelette. It wasn't Morgan's fault that Vera had chosen this moment to call. She shouldn't have to eat cold food.

'I asked you a question, Jason.' Vera was beginning to sound hysterical.

'Look,' he said, 'this really isn't a good time.'

'Jason, please—'

'Some other time,' he said abruptly and put down the phone.

The phone rang again, but this time Jason ignored it. When it stopped Morgan said, 'I'm sorry, but I couldn't help overhearing—trouble of some sort?'

Jason looked across the table at her. Morgan's eyes were clear and her gaze steady, interested but not inquisitive. She had the look of a woman in whom a man could confide. Jason was almost tempted to tell her about Vera and the demands she kept making on him. Almost... But not quite.

'Trouble?' He shrugged. 'Nothing I can't deal with.'

She smiled at him. 'As long as it's not serious.'

'Annoying, that's all.' Jason drank the last of his coffee and stood up. 'Have to be off.'

He was about to leave the kitchen when Morgan said, 'Last night, Jason, you said something about a fence.'

He pushed a hand through his glossy dark hair. 'That's right. Fence-breaks are never good news and, from what one of the men said, this sounds like a bad one. Pity we're short-handed today.'

'Are you going to repair it by yourself, Jason?'

'Won't know till I see it. One way or another, I'll do my best.'

'I'll help you.' Morgan's offer was impulsive.

Jason stared at her disbelievingly. 'You?'

'I once spent a summer at the cash-desk of a hardware

store. In the process I learned to swing a hammer, as well as several other useful skills.' She grinned at his incredulous expression. 'I can see you don't believe me.'

'You're absolutely right.'

'I won't bother calling you a chauvinist again.'

This time her smile robbed the words of their sting. 'Good,' Jason said, grinning back.

'You won't believe this either, but I do many of the repairs in my apartment.'

'There must be twenty adoring men who'd gladly do them for you.' He was speaking only partly in jest.

'Twenty?' Morgan wrinkled her nose at him. 'Haven't counted lately.'

She was teasing, of course, yet Jason was willing to bet that Morgan really did have a string of willing males she could call on whenever the need arose.

'I really think I could help you with the fence,' she said.

Jason's eyes went to her fragile arms. 'Thanks for the offer but, no,' he said.

'Let me come with you at least.'

'No, Morgan.'

'It would give me a chance to see another part of the ranch.'

Jason tried to ignore the sense of sheer pleasure that came over him at the idea of a morning with Morgan at his side. He shook his head.

She couldn't leave it at that. 'Please let me come. Please, Jason.'

It was the 'Please, Jason' that got to him. At that moment Jason was glad that he hadn't told Morgan about his problems with Vera. In the end they were the same, Vera and Morgan—it wasn't the first time he had thought that. Both women were so persistent in their demands, never letting go of a man until they had what they wanted.

'You must have other things to do,' he said curtly.

This time he didn't wait for Morgan to tell him what she thought of a man who considered that a woman ought to confine herself to 'womanly activities'. His expression was grim as he left the house.

'What are you doing here?' Jason demanded ten minutes later when Morgan walked into the stables.

'I'm going with you.' It was a statement this time, not a plea.

His eyes were hard. 'I've already said no. I don't need your help, Morgan.'

'Let me come anyway.' She smiled up at him. 'I hate the idea of spending a day at the ranch-house when I could be out on the range. I don't have much time left at the ranch. Brent will be back soon and you'll see the back of me after that.'

There was such spirit and eagerness in Morgan's tone. Jason's gaze went from her shining eyes and uptilted mouth to a body that seemed to have been made for caressing. Morgan's time at the ranch was passing quickly. Jason already knew that his life would be empty without her.

He felt his muscles contract as Morgan put her hand on his arm. 'You've been angry since that phone call. I don't know what it was about, but I wish you wouldn't take your anger out on me.'

She was too perceptive. If he wasn't careful she would be guessing his innermost thoughts and emotions.

'Since you're so determined,' he said at last, 'and only because it's true that you'll be gone soon, you can come.'

Blue eyes sparkled mischievously. 'I accept that very gracious invitation. Thank you, Jason.'

Aloofly he looked down at her. 'Go get your gear,' he said gruffly.

'It's outside the stables.'

'So you brought your riding things with you from the house?'

She gave him a saucy look. 'Nothing wrong with that.'

'Depends on how you view a person who must have her way all the time.' His tone was flat.

In that sense she was like his ex-wife, Jason thought grimly. Morgan and Vera, two women cast in the same mould—bent on getting what they wanted, no matter what the consequences.

Yet there was a difference, one that Jason recognized despite his annoyance. Vera was ugly when she wanted something, shrill and given to whining. Morgan, on the other hand, was gorgeous. Her eyes shone with amusement and her cheeks were rosy with colour. Morgan might go all out to get what she wanted, but she would never stoop to whining while she did so.

Which did not make her any easier to deal with.

They had been riding for more than an hour when they came to the fence. As Jason began to study the break Morgan dismounted, careful this time to tether Mayhem securely.

'Bad?' she asked, coming up beside him.

'Bad enough,' he muttered.

'Can it be fixed?'

'Has to be. See those ragged edges? A stray calf could get badly injured. I'd like to do something about it right now before there's an accident.'

'But?' Morgan asked, evidently hearing the word in his voice.

'That kind of break can't be fixed by just one person. I need someone to help me.' His expression was sombre. 'Much as I hate to leave it like this, I'll have to come back later with one of the men.'

'I've already offered to help you,' Morgan said.

'Don't even think about it.' He didn't turn his eyes from the fence as he spoke.

'I mean it, Jason.'

He did look up then. 'It's a ridiculous idea, Morgan.' But there was a glimmer of a question in his eyes.

'No, Jason, you know it isn't.' Once more that hand was on his arm. Preoccupied as Jason was, the soft touch sent shock waves through his system.

'Think about it,' Morgan coaxed. 'It could save one of your calves from getting hurt. Please let me help, Jason.'

This was a different 'Please, Jason.' Earlier he had thought she might have her own motives for wanting to go riding with him, but this was a genuine offer of help. Jason's eyes flicked over Morgan's face, lingering for a long moment on lips that tempted him madly every time he looked at them.

'What do you think you can do?' he asked abruptly.

'Hold up the broken part of the fence while you work on it. Maybe do a bit of fixing alongside you.'

As Jason hesitated Morgan's lovely laughter rang out on the hot air. 'I can see you still don't believe that I can use tools.'

'Can you really?' Jason sounded unconvinced.

'Wouldn't say so if I couldn't.' Softly she added, 'You seem to have some odd ideas about women. We're a lot more than decorative objects. More than people who only know how to cook and clean and raise babies. Hard as it may be for you to believe, there are other things we can do well.'

'Obviously you still think I'm a chauvinist,' Jason said drily.

'You said it this time—I didn't.' But Morgan was smiling.

Jason gave it one last try. 'Fixing fences isn't what you were hired to do at the ranch.'

She laughed again. 'As usual, you're looking for ways to put me off. I *want* to help, Jason.'

Jason looked down at her—a fragile figure in Vera's riding-pants, tightly belted because they were too big for her. Her blouse, damp from the heat, clung to her alluringly so that he could make out her breasts beneath the thin fabric. From beneath the broad-brimmed hat her eyes sparkled up at him, wide and blue, spirited and amused.

'Will you let me help, Jason?'

In the end he did.

The repairs took quite a while. Now and then Morgan caught Jason looking at her, his expression quizzical. Each time she would shoot him a saucy look in return.

'You seem to be having a good time,' he said once.

'Even better than you realize.'

In fact, she seemed to be enjoying every second. Jason tried, without success, to picture Vera working on the fence in the scorching heat and managing to look cheerful as well as enchanting. It made no sense that a girl who was so unaccustomed to the rigours of ranch life could be so different from his ex-wife.

'There's so much I don't know about you,' he said musingly.

Morgan looked at him. 'I don't know much about you either.'

'Will you have supper with me tonight, Morgan?' Jason surprised himself by asking the question.

'We eat together every night.'

'In town. I know a decent restaurant.'

She danced him a sparkling grin. 'Payment for my help with the fence?'

'An evening out. A chance to talk.'

An extra sparkle appeared in Morgan's eyes, but when she spoke her tone was light. 'I'd like that,' she said.

And so later that evening, after Morgan had finished in the cookhouse, they took the Jeep and drove to a restaurant in the little town that bordered the ranch on one side.

The food was delicious: butter-soft Texas steak, some intriguing baked vegetables and a tangy salad. Jason knew about wines. He didn't hesitate long over the wine list, and the one he chose complemented the food perfectly.

Good as the meal was, the conversation was even better. Away from the ranch and on neutral ground, so to speak, they were—perhaps for the first time since they had met—able to talk without restraint.

Morgan listened attentively while Jason told her about his early days at Six-Gate Corral. He had been born on the ranch, and had spent his youth learning every aspect of the business. There had been lean years, difficult years, during one of which Jason's father had died. It had taken hard work and tenacity before Jason had turned things around and made the ranch the successful operation it was now.

And then it was Jason's turn to listen. He listened quietly, and without much pleasure, as Morgan told him about her career. One thing became clearer every minute. It was impossible that their worlds could ever meet— even if he wanted them to. Which he did not. It was dangerous even to think about it.

They begin to talk of other things—music and sport and what was happening in the world—and they were amazed to find that, although their backgrounds were different, they still had interests in common.

It was quite late when they left the restaurant, unwilling to end the evening yet knowing that they had no option because the working day began so early. In not too many hours Jason would be riding his horse on the range, and Morgan would be in the cookhouse preparing food for the men.

They walked to the Jeep, not quite touching yet so close that they were acutely aware of each other. Each felt a deep and hungry longing—one that cried out to be fulfilled.

As Jason leaned across Morgan to open the door of the Jeep his arm brushed against her breast. For a timeless moment they both stood quite still. Jason's arm was warm and strong, and Morgan's nipples sprang to instant, throbbing life. Jason's breathing was suddenly shallow.

He was moving towards Morgan when she looked up at him, her lips slightly parted. 'Jason?' she whispered. 'Jason, please…'

Jason, please. The words he had heard a few times already that day. From Vera, with her selfish demands. From Morgan, with demands of another kind. How could he have forgotten?

Morgan was no less a threat than Vera. If anything, she was more dangerous because her loveliness had lulled him into letting down his guard. She looked at you with those big blue eyes and made you feel that you wanted to drown in them; smiled at you with those sweetly curved lips, and had you thinking that what you wanted more than anything in the world was to kiss them.

He had come very close tonight to saying things that he had never said to any woman. When Morgan returned to her real life she would laugh at those things with her city friends—at the things the simple rancher had felt and said.

Abruptly he moved from the door. A second later Morgan was sliding uncomprehendingly along the seat.

In the Jeep on the way back to the ranch the strain was intense. Jason sat very upright, his hands clenched tightly on the steering-wheel. Morgan sat at the other end of the seat. After a fleeting look at her unhappy face Jason didn't look at her again. They drove all the way in silence.

Back at the ranch-house, Jason parked the Jeep. As they walked to the house not a trace remained of the togetherness they had shared. They were two people who happened to have spent an evening together. Two strangers, keeping a deliberate distance from each other.

They came into the house and Jason said, 'Goodnight.' His tone was impersonal.

'Goodnight,' Morgan responded, her tone low and sounding close to tears.

Don't cry, Jason pleaded silently, knowing that he would not be able to stand it if she did.

He was walking away from her when she called him back. 'Jason…'

He turned. 'Yes?'

'What is it? What's wrong?'

Jason stiffened. He should have expected the question, should have been ready for it. 'Nothing.'

'That's not true,' Morgan said urgently. 'Jason, what happened?'

Jason forced a shrug. He could sense a scene brewing, Vera had made enough scenes to last him a lifetime, and he wasn't in the mood for another. Especially not with Morgan.

'It's late,' he said coolly, 'and we both have to be up early.'

'I will not go to bed until you've told me what's wrong!'

Jason was feeling tenser by the moment. It had been a mistake to invite Morgan to have dinner with him, just

as he shouldn't have given in and let her go with him
to the fence that morning.

'Don't you understand?' he said irritably. 'I wish you
wouldn't keep on about nothing.'

'But there is something! Why are you being so eva-
sive? We had a lovely evening. A *wonderful* evening.
We were getting on so well, Jason. It was only when we
got to the car that…that things changed. Did I do something to offend you?'

You made me want you. You almost made me forget
that we can never belong together. And the way you
looked at me and said, 'Jason, please…'

'Don't go on with this, Morgan.'

'If it was something I did…said…' There was a little
catch in her voice.

It was dark in the hallway but a light, shining in the
living-room, made it possible for Jason to see Morgan's
face. Her lips trembled slightly, and in her eyes tears
shimmered. Morgan's face, small and vulnerable, was
the sweetest thing Jason had ever seen.

He ached to take her in his arms, to hold her and chase
the tears from her eyes. To love her… *No*! The word
made him flinch. He did *not* love her, and never would.

Without realizing what he was doing, he had taken a
step towards her. Now he drew back deliberately.

'You're making a drama out of nothing,' he said
harshly. 'We had a pleasant evening—can't you leave it
at that?'

A few seconds passed. Jason waited tensely.

And then Morgan's shoulders straightened and her
chin lifted. 'I'm glad nothing's wrong,' she said brightly.
'Thanks for a nice evening. As you say, it was…
pleasant. Goodnight, Jason.'

When Morgan returned from the cookhouse the next
morning Jason was in the kitchen.

'Good morning,' she said.

'Hi,' he responded shortly.

Usually they ate breakfast together, but today Jason had not waited for her. 'You've already eaten, I see,' she said.

Jason nodded. 'I'm in a hurry to get going.'

He drained his coffee and left the room, leaving Morgan with the uncomfortable feeling that he might have spent more time over his meal if she had not arrived when she had.

Standing at the window and watching him walk purposefully in the direction of the stables, Morgan wished that she understood him. With every passing day she loved him more deeply. His strength, his toughness, the heart-rending tenderness she glimpsed in him now and then. The wonderful dark eyes in the rugged face. The incredible sexiness which often drove her wild with a longing she had never experienced with any other man.

But there was the other side of him as well—unreasonable, implacable and impatient when she least expected it. Something had happened to change Jason's mood last night and it had been obvious that he hadn't wanted to talk about it. For much of the night she had lain sleepless, thinking about it.

Suddenly Morgan's sense of pride asserted itself. She loved Jason, but her feelings were clearly not reciprocated. She had tried her best to talk to him but without success. She would be a fool if she spent the rest of the day eating her heart out over him.

When the phone rang some time later, and she heard the voice of her favourite photographer at the other end of the line, she was glad.

'Morgan, hi. Hope my timing isn't bad?'

'Oh, Stan, hi. Your timing's not bad at all. On the contrary, I needed a friendly soul to speak to.'

'Are they treating you badly out on the ranch?' He sounded concerned.

'Pretty well, actually.' Morgan decided against baring her heart to Stan. 'I guess I'm just feeling a bit sorry for myself.' This wasn't the first time Stan had phoned, and she knew what he wanted to talk about. 'You're calling about your portfolio.'

'Right. Sorry to bug you, Morgan, but I have a deadline to meet, and I need to know which photos you want me to select. It would mean a lot to me to have some of your pictures in my portfolio.'

'I know,' she said remorsefully. 'I should have got my suggestions to you long ago. My only excuse is that I've been busy on the ranch... But I'll get out the catalogue and start working on it right away.'

'When will I hear from you, Morgan?'

'End of the week be OK?'

'Can you make it sooner?'

Morgan was feeling more than a little guilty about procrastinating for so long. 'I'll try and mail something to you tomorrow morning,' she promised.

When she had put down the phone she went to her room and fetched the store's advertising catalogue.

Her forehead puckered in thought as she studied the three pages of swimsuit photos. Which ones should she suggest that Stan include in the portfolio he was compiling? The choices were more difficult than she had expected. Slowly, thoughtfully, she began to make notes.

It was early afternoon when she looked at the time. In an hour or so the men would be returning from the range, hungry, tired and expecting a hearty meal. But she hadn't yet finished the work for Stan.

She decided to take the catalogue with her to the cookhouse. There were often chunks of time when she was not actually doing something. While she waited for water to boil or potatoes to cook she could go on writing.

She would make sure that she put the catalogue away safely before the men came to eat.

There were a dozen pictures in all, each one capturing a different mood. Morgan looking playful in a candy-striped swimsuit, one hand holding a brightly coloured beachball, while in another picture she was sleekly elegant in jade. There was the sexy pose in the red bikini—two tiny strips of fabric alluringly revealing long slim legs and the swell of her breasts—while a strand of hair was caught between her teeth.

And there was the romantic picture in which a pair of bronze male arms were folded around her, fingertips resting just beneath her breasts. Morgan's eyes rested longest on this picture as she remembered how long it had taken to get the pose right. The bronze arms belonged to a man called Damian. She had worked with Damian before, a man who was so imbued with his movie-star appearance that Morgan sometimes wondered whether he could ever be in love with anyone but himself.

The way Damian held her and Morgan's own dreamy-eyed look were meant to suggest passion. In fact, there hadn't been any. As with most modelling, there had been only hours and hours of posing on a hot California day with the ocean as a backdrop. Posing until Morgan would have liked to have called the whole thing off, but couldn't because this was her livelihood. Passion, she thought now, was not a pair of arms belonging to a bored male model who would have been far happier doing something else.

Passion was a rugged man with muscles like steel who held you close to his throbbing body and ignited flames in your own. Passion was the wild urge to make love with that man—to bury your fingers in his hair and explore his body, to kiss and kiss for ever...

Morgan gave herself a small mental shake. She should

know by now that passion with Jason was impossible because Jason, for reasons known only to himself, didn't want it to happen.

A hissing kettle drew her attention back to the stove. It was time to put away the catalogue and go back to her cooking.

When the cowboys began to filter into the cookhouse she was ready for them. They were at ease with her now, even some of the shyer ones who had avoided her at the start. As always, she thought what a nice lot they were, not only Charlie—who was at her side whenever he could be—but the rest of them as well. All of them were thoroughly attractive men—except Hank, and she had got into the habit of ignoring him.

They sat down at the long cookhouse table and began to eat. Morgan was always careful now to cook huge quantities of food. These days there was almost always praise for her cooking. 'Won't be the same when Brent gets back,' Charlie said, and many of the other cowboys echoed the comment.

Morgan couldn't have said quite when she became conscious of an odd silence in the cookhouse. Some of the men were staring in one direction, their expressions peculiar. There was nervousness in the air and also an indefinable aura of excitement. Aware of a sudden prickling of the hair at the back of her neck, Morgan made herself look in the same direction as the men.

Hank was holding court at one end of the cookhouse. Morgan's catalogue was open in his hands. A few of the bolder cowboys had gathered around him and he was teasing them, letting them have brief glimpses of the catalogue before clutching it to his chest.

In a second Morgan was rigid. Every inch of her body felt cold. She felt as if she was in the midst of some dreadful nightmare, one from which she would surely wake. It was impossible that Hank could have found the catalogue—she remembered putting it away safely before the men arrived in the cookhouse. But there was no waking from this dream. Hank was real, and so was the catalogue in his hands. And she had to find a way of getting it back.

Seconds later she was confronting him. 'Give that to me!'

'Sure, pretty lady.' The cowboy's eyes were hot, his expression lascivious in a way she had seen before. 'Sure, I'll give it to you—in the bunkhouse.'

There was no mistaking what he meant. Cold gave way to heat as a flush stained Morgan's cheeks. Inside her a great trembling had started, yet she had the presence of mind to understand that it would not do for Hank to know that she was frightened.

'Give it to me now!' she ordered.

'You heard me, pretty lady. In the bunkhouse. In my bed.'

'Give it to her.' Charlie's voice, close beside her.

'Keep out of this, pipsqueak,' Hank mocked.

Morgan made a sudden lunge for the catalogue, but Hank was quicker than she was. Thrusting the catalogue behind his back, he dared her to make another try for it.

'Give it to me this instant,' Morgan said, with all the authority she could muster.

But Hank only laughed—an ugly laugh, loud and obscene in the eerily silent cookhouse. 'You know the terms, pretty lady. You can have your pictures back—in my bed, enjoying what I have to give you.'

Morgan felt thoroughly ill as she saw the way his eyes ravaged her—blatantly, insolently—making no effort to hide his intentions.

'Why wouldn't I give you the pictures?' the cowboy jeered. 'I don't need them. Prefer the real thing in my hands any time.'

'Quit it, Hank!' a furious voice shouted. It was Charlie again.

But Hank ignored the quieter, smaller, gentler man. 'Come to my bunk, Morgan,' he wheedled. 'I'll give you the best time you ever had. You won't miss lover-boy here.' He stabbed a finger at the picture of the male model. 'So, how about it, sweetheart?'

At the start of Hank's outrage only a few of the cowboys had gathered around him. Most of the others had remained at the table, as if they were stunned by what was happening and more than a little embarrassed. They all liked Morgan. But Hank was popular too, a natural leader, respected by the men for his fearlessness and daring. They didn't know what to make of what was happening and weren't certain how they should react.

Gradually, however, the atmosphere in the cookhouse was beginning to change. One by one the cowboys left the table until soon they were all crowding around Morgan and Hank.

Hank was fully aware of the interest he had created. Bully and showman that he was, he enjoyed the attention. Turning to his pals, he smacked his lips. 'Hey, Bud, Stuey, come look at these pictures.' Another smack of the lips. 'Some body, eh? Enough to make a fellow drool. And just asking to be taken.'

'I'm warning you!' Charlie shouted.

'Warning me of what?' Hank dismissed him easily. 'What do you think you can do, little boy?' And, to the other cowboys, he said, 'This is some doll, guys. Hey, Morgan, look what you and I will do in my bunk.' With that he kissed the pictures, all the time keeping his eyes blatantly on her.

She was rigid once more, not with fear now—in spite of everything, she wasn't intimidated by Hank—but with revulsion and distaste.

'Ready to go to my bunk, pretty lady?'

Clearly Hank was not about to give back the catalogue. The more she pleaded with him the happier he would be. She couldn't give him that satisfaction. In fact, the only way she could put an end to the scene was by distancing herself from it.

She was determined to get back her catalogue but she would have to wait until later, until things had calmed somewhat, to do it.

She was about to leave the cookhouse when the noise level suddenly rose. With a sinking heart Morgan looked back.

Charlie, enraged beyond all reason, had taken a swing at Hank. It was not the first time he had tried to defend her honour, but this was far worse than anything that gone before. A fight erupted in seconds. Charlie was punching and swinging with all his might but Hank, stronger and already aroused by the pictures, was the more aggressive of the two and certainly the more vicious.

God, this was awful! 'Do something,' Morgan pleaded. She tugged at the shirt of one cowboy and at the arm of another. 'You have to do something. *Stop the fight!*' But the men ignored her.

It was left to the strongest and angriest of the lot to end it. Drawn by the noise to the cookhouse, Jason instantly took in what was happening. Quickly he pulled the two adversaries apart.

'Thank God you came when you did!' Pale and on the verge of tears, Morgan was at Jason's side.

He looked down at her. Though he had yet to learn the cause of the fight, given the personalities involved it was not difficult to guess that Morgan had had something to do with it.

'Get out of here,' he ordered.

'Jason, I—'

'Now!' he said roughly, seizing her arm and walking her to the doorway of the cookhouse.

'You don't understand… I only—'

'Out, Morgan!'

'Hank has my catalogue. I have to have it. I—'

'I don't know what the hell you're talking about, but I want you out of here,' he said grimly. *'Now.'*

Morgan heard his tone. For once there was nothing for it but to do as he ordered without further argument.

CHAPTER SEVEN

'HANK won't be bothering you again.'

Morgan looked at Jason as he walked into the ranch-house. A little while had passed since he had ordered her out of the cookhouse. Uneasily she had wandered from one room to another, too restless to settle down to anything. Even the suggestions for Stan would have to wait until she felt calmer than she did now. Besides, she could do nothing until she got back the catalogue.

'Hank apologized?' she asked incredulously.

'Apologize? Hank?' Jason's laugh was short and hard. 'You must be kidding!'

'I only thought...'

'What did you think?' His tone lashed her. Morgan saw that his face was tight, the skin stretched tautly over the high cheek-bones.

'I thought that maybe... Well, you did say that Hank won't be bothering me again. How can you be so certain?' She flinched as Jason tossed the catalogue at her. 'You got it back!'

'Yes, Morgan, I did. It's torn because Charlie tussled with Hank, trying to get it away from him. Just as well the other men didn't manage to lay their hands on it. Think how they'd have loved these naked pictures.'

'Not in one single picture am I naked,' Morgan defended herself indignantly.

'Oh, no? I'd say you don't compare too badly with some of the pin-ups the men have on the walls of the bunkhouse.'

'That's not fair,' Morgan whispered. Her face was

very pale suddenly and her lips quivered. 'Pin-ups are a deliberate turn-on.'

'And these aren't?' He made a savage gesture.

'No,' she said, 'they are not.' It was difficult to speak firmly when she was so distressed, but Morgan knew that she had to try. 'These are fashion photographs, Jason. They're meant for women, showing the latest in swimsuit fashions. They were never meant to be pin-ups.'

'Fashions with sexual overtones.' Jason's tone was derisive.

'Only one or two of them. Besides, it's the way the industry works.'

'Really? Well, maybe you don't want to know what I think of your industry. Or of the people who work in it.' Jason's voice was contemptuous.

'You condemn a world you know nothing about because a crude, horrible man caused a rumpus.' Morgan's voice shook.

She had been feeling ill since the moment she had seen the catalogue in Hank's hands, and she felt even worse now. She wanted only to go to her room—to get away from the eyes that looked at her with such loathing and from the voice that tore at her with every word Jason spoke. Morgan didn't care too much what Hank thought of her, but the opinion of Jason—the man she loved— did matter. It hurt to know how much he despised her.

'About Hank…' she said hesitantly.

'You won't see him at Six-Gate Corral again.'

'I still don't know… He decided to leave?'

'I fired him,' Jason said curtly.

Morgan stared at him incredulously. 'Because of me?' she asked at last.

'Because of what happened. And don't flatter yourself, Morgan. Don't think I was out to defend your honour. I'm not some shining knight, riding out of the sunset on his charger. I'm not your doting Charlie.'

'Then why?' she whispered.

Dark eyes rested on her face for a long moment. They moved downwards over her throat and her breasts beneath the soft T-shirt. Downwards further—over her hips and thighs. It was a blatantly searching gaze, a gaze that made no attempt to hide its scorn. A gaze that seemed to strip her naked and defenceless.

Morgan took a quick step backwards. Without thinking, her hands lifted and closed protectively over her breasts.

'Don't look at me like that!' she cried.

'Spare me, Morgan. Don't you think that, in the circumstances, this modest behaviour is more than a little ridiculous? Besides, what are you trying to hide? That luscious figure of yours? Why bother—when it's on public display all the time?'

'It isn't on display, at least not in the hateful way you're implying. Modelling is part of my job at the store, Jason. You always knew that. I'm paid to show off clothes to their best advantage. Not my body—definitely not that.'

As Jason's expression remained as scornful as ever Morgan raised her head and straightened her shoulders. 'You seem to think I should be ashamed of what I do. I'm not! I'm *proud* of my career. Do you understand, Jason? *Proud.*'

Deliberately she dropped her hands from her breasts, and lifted her head even higher. 'Getting back to Hank, you haven't told me why you fired him.'

'He was disruptive, and I can't employ a man who fights. By rights, I should have fired Charlie too.'

'No, Jason, not Charlie! Please, not Charlie!'

'He threw the first punch. That much is quite clear by all accounts.'

'He only acted in my defence.'

'Poor misguided fool,' Jason sneered. 'No, Morgan, you can rest easy. Your precious Charlie's position is still secure. Hank… Hank didn't know when to stop, and there's no way that both men could have remained here. With emotions running so high, there'd have been another fight sooner or later—with or without your presence at Six-Gate Corral. I don't tolerate fighting on this ranch, Morgan. I've told you that before.'

Morgan made a small helpless gesture. 'You're well rid of Hank.'

'What do you know about it?' Jason demanded, rounding on her. There was steel in his eyes and jaw, and his expression was dangerous.

'I got to know the man.'

'One side of him. Only one side—remember that, Morgan. After what happened I had no choice but to get rid of him, but don't think I'm happy about it. Hank was one of the best cowboys on this ranch.'

'I get the feeling,' she said unhappily, 'that you blame me for everything that happened.'

'Shouldn't I?' he asked aloofly.

Morgan didn't answer him immediately. She looked at the tall figure: at the long muscular body, power in every inch; at the hard-boned face, the tight lips and jaw; at eyes that could warm with amusement, and were now filled with dislike and disapproval. Despite the heat, she felt very cold.

'I warned you it could happen, Morgan. That first night, after the uproar in the cookhouse, and then later when I ordered you out of the bunkhouse.'

'Jason—'

'I warned you,' he said relentlessly. 'I said the men might resort to fighting over you. I asked you to leave the ranch—more than once—but you had your contract. That bloody watertight contract that Brent should never have given you. You knew you weren't welcome, Morgan, but you insisted on staying, no matter what I said.' His eyes glittered. 'The moment I walked into the cookhouse and saw what was happening I knew, without asking, that the men had to be fighting over little Miss Morgan Muir.'

His disgust made her feel ill. 'If only Hank had never seen those pictures,' she said in a low voice.

'If only,' Jason countered derisively. 'The question is, how did the catalogue get to the cookhouse?' And as Morgan looked at him uncertainly, he added, 'I can't see Hank stealing into your room and finding it there. Not even Hank would take a chance like that.'

'No...'

'You took it to the cookhouse, didn't you, Morgan?'

A small tongue went out to wet lips that were suddenly dry. 'You don't understand, Jason. You see—'

'Yes or no?' he demanded harshly.

'Yes... But—'

'So it was deliberate. You took a dozen sexy pictures to a bunch of men who don't get to see women as often as they should. Men without wives, most of them without steady girlfriends. You must have known the effect those pictures would have on them.'

'I didn't think about it. You see—'

Jason didn't let her finish. 'You *must* have known what would happen.' He bit out the words and hurled them at her. 'It isn't as if you're some innocent little virgin, Morgan. You're a big-city woman, sophisticated and accustomed to seeing what her lovely body does to a man. How it inflames him, excites him.'

'Stop!' she pleaded.

But a furious Jason would not be stopped so easily. 'A cookhouse full of cowboys. Strong men, easily aroused. The first night when you got into that bed in the bunkhouse—I asked you what you were after. I gave you the benefit of the doubt then. This time I insist on knowing if you were trying to inflame the men. Well, sexy Morgan?'

'Of course not!' she whispered, sick and appalled.

'I believe that just once before you finally leave this ranch you wanted to see the effect you could have on the men—wanted to be turned on by their excitement. Wanted to enjoy your siren powers over a bunch of helpless cowboys. *That's* why you took the catalogue to the cookhouse.'

'I refuse to listen to this!'

Morgan had, in fact, been feeling more than a little guilty. She had been so certain that she had put the catalogue in a safe place before the men appeared for their meal. Was it possible that she could have been mistaken?

That guilt was now joined by a rage that equalled Jason's. 'You have no right to talk to me like this! No right at all! You don't even understand what happened!'

Turning, she walked quickly to the door—intent only on putting distance between herself and Jason. When he came up behind her, seized her arm and spun her around she gasped.

'Let go of me,' she snarled. 'I've had all I can take.'

She tried to get away from him, but his grip on her arm tightened. 'Which of the cowboys were you after, Morgan? Charlie? Hank? Or was it someone else?'

'Stop it!' she cried. 'I refuse to listen to this!'

'Which one, Morgan?'

'I don't have to take any more of this!' she shouted.

'Which one, lovely Morgan?'

His fingers bit hard into her soft skin, bringing tears to Morgan's eyes. For a long moment they stared at each other, both tense with anger and both breathing hard.

'Let go of me, Jason!' Morgan ordered.

'When I'm ready to,' he said, and pulled her closer.

His face was inches from hers now, so close that she could feel his warm breath on her cheeks. He was about to kiss her, she knew. So many times she had longed for him to do just this. But not in anger, not in punishment.

'Let me go!' she cried again.

'If I don't, will you use your famous self-defence skills on me?' Jason taunted.

The jeering tone, as much as the inflammatory words, got to her. It was all too much—first Hank humiliating her and now Jason condemning her beyond endurance.

Suddenly Morgan was back in the self-defence class she had attended in Austin. She saw the classroom, with its bare walls and padded floors, and the instructor, stocky and uncompromising—down to earth with those women who questioned whether they would ever be able to put their new skills into effect. 'When you have to, you will remember what you've been taught,' he had said.

Morgan remembered.

As Jason pulled her even closer she moved. Her right leg curled around Jason's right leg. Her foot lifted, her calf connecting with his. She heard his hissing exclamation as his leg rose involuntarily in the air at the same time as her right hand pushed hard against his chest. A second later he was flat on the floor.

'*Good Lord*!' He stared up at her, so taken aback that Morgan laughed.

A moment later, realizing what she had done, she was bending over him. 'Did I hurt you?'

'My pride, more than anything else.'

'You asked for it, Jason. I refuse to apologize.'

'I'm not asking you to.'

Incredibly, now that the first moment of shock had passed a sparkle was in his eyes and his lips tilted. And then his expression changed again.

As he stood up he reached for her. This time she could not resist. She wanted him so much.

His kisses were hard, passionate, and she was kissing him too. All she felt now was desire—hot, pulsating and throbbing deep inside her. Without knowing what she was doing, she moaned softly deep in her throat. She wanted this man, yearned for him; her whole body was on fire for him.

Suddenly Jason raised his head. 'Who is he, Morgan?' And as she looked at him uncomprehendingly, still dazed from their kisses, he continued, 'The man in the pictures. The one with his hands on your body.'

Such an unimportant question. 'He's a model,' Morgan said.

'His name?'

'Damian.'

'Damian.' The word was spoken with utter loathing. 'What is this Damian to you, Morgan?'

In that moment it came to her—*Jason was jealous*. He had no reason to be jealous, but she wouldn't tell him that. He didn't deserve to know, not after he had condemned her so unfairly.

'What do you care?' she taunted.

'Answer me, Morgan. Who is this man? This model? Did you make love with him?'

'What do you think, Jason?'

A second later Jason answered his own question. 'Yes, I think—I know—you made love.'

'Think whatever you like.' She was still taunting him.

'Why did you come here without him? No wonder you're after the cowboys—you must be missing your Damian.'

'Think whatever you like,' Morgan said through tight lips.

'You're shameless. Totally shameless.' Jason's face was filled with disgust.

He took a few steps away her, then turned back. 'If
only you weren't so beautiful,' he muttered hoarsely.

'What are you saying, Jason?'

'The most beautiful woman in the world.' A second
later he added, 'Forget I said that.'

'Jason—'

'It didn't mean anything,' he denied savagely.

He was at the door when Morgan called him back. He
turned his head. 'Well?' he bit out.

'It's time I went.'

Was it her imagination or did the rugged face go a
little pale beneath the tan? But Jason remained silent.

'It's true that I stayed when I knew you didn't want
me here. I should have known that I couldn't...
couldn't...' Morgan hesitated, waiting until she was certain that she could keep the tearfulness from her voice.

'What I'm saying,' she went on, 'is that I'll leave the
ranch. I'll go in the morning. You'll be able to forget
that I was ever here.'

'That,' Jason said brusquely, 'will be difficult.'

A minute later Morgan heard the slam of the back
door and the sound of angry footsteps on the path that
led around the house. Not long after that there was the
sound of a horse's hooves, galloping away from the stables.

Only now did Morgan go to her room. Flinging herself on her bed, she wept as if her heart would break.
This, then, was how it was all going to end.

There was a knock at the door.

Morgan was busy, closing her suitcase. Outside it was
still dark, but soon the eastern sky would be grey with
the light of early dawn and another day would begin at
Six-Gate Corral.

There was another knock. And then a voice called,
'Morgan? Open up.'

Morgan turned the key in the lock of the case and composed her expression, before opening the door. She didn't want Jason to know that she had spent much of the night weeping.

Stiffly she said, 'Why so impatient, Jason? Can't wait to see me leave, I guess? Well, I'll go soon enough. Only...' She stopped, hoping that she wouldn't cry once more.

'Only?' he prompted. His eyes were on her face and his tone was so odd.

'The men will be coming to the cookhouse soon, and they'll be upset when they find there's no breakfast. I... Well, I'd like to be there, Jason.'

'To cook a last meal for them?'

'That—and to say goodbye.' She looked away from him, away from a face that would be imprinted on her mind for the rest of her life.

She braced herself for a sarcastic comment. But Jason was silent, and in a way that was more unnerving than anything he could have said.

Morgan forced herself to look back at him, her voice unsteady when she spoke again. 'They won't be surprised to hear that I'm leaving, not after yesterday. But I'd hate to go without talking to them.' Her eyes pleaded for understanding. 'Please, Jason, I want very badly to say goodbye to the cowboys.'

'That won't be necessary.' Again there was that odd tone.

Morgan stared at him disbelievingly. 'You won't let me talk to them? I don't believe it! You're a hard man, Jason, but even you can't be as hard as that. Or as cynical. I didn't try to seduce the cowboys, Jason. I never set out to inflame them—whatever you may think. Besides, how much harm do you think I could possibly cause in a few minutes?'

'A bundle-full.' Unexpectedly, Jason was grinning.

'You can cause harm without meaning to, Morgan Muir, as I've learned to my cost.'

Her head jerked, and for some reason the blood flowed a little faster in her veins. 'I don't understand.'

'Don't you?' Still that grin.

'Of course not! I don't have the slightest idea what you're talking about. Please let me say my goodbyes, Jason. You can come with me, watch me every second and make certain I don't do the wrong thing.'

The dark eyes were watching her intently. 'No goodbyes, Morgan. At least not yet—not until Brent gets back.'

As the full meaning of his words made their impact, Morgan gasped. '*What are you saying*?'

'I was down at the bunkhouse last night. I guessed that the men would be unsettled, what with the fight and with Hank having to leave the ranch. They seemed glad to see me. They wanted to talk. All of them, Morgan, not just Charlie.'

'They talked about Hank?' Morgan asked, and held her breath.

'And about you, Morgan. I learned that your catalogue was hidden under a pile of recipe files, where nobody should have found it. Apparently, Hank had been delving around in your things. He found the catalogue and discovered the pictures. He boasted about it to the guys afterwards before he was fired.'

'I was so certain I'd put it away…'

'You had, and I wouldn't let you speak.'

Jason's expression was sombre. He fell silent and Morgan had the feeling that his thoughts had turned inward and that he did not like their drift.

At length he said, 'The men want you to stay, Morgan. I'm here to pass on the message.'

A great surge of emotion filled her chest and behind

her lids the treacherous tears once more pricked. But all she said was, 'I see.'

Jason gestured towards the suitcase. 'Meanwhile, you're all packed.' He paused a moment, and Morgan saw him swallow. 'I said some terrible things yesterday, Morgan—I'm sorry.'

Sorry... The word sounded so strange coming from Jason. As if the apology had been reluctantly torn from him.

'I think you meant some of those things,' she said slowly.

His expression was distant. 'Some of them, yes,' he said, and Morgan knew that he still thought badly of her modelling.

He looked once more at her suitcase. 'I've told you what I had to—the men want you to stay.'

'And you, Jason?' Morgan asked softly. 'Do *you* want it too?'

The lids came down over his eyes, and the hard lines of his face tightened. 'Yes,' he said at length, so abruptly that Morgan knew the word was also torn from him. 'I do.'

For a few seconds they stood staring at each other. Morgan had the strangest feeling that it would not take much to close the distance that separated them. If that happened there might be no breakfast for the cowboys that morning. But Jason didn't move, nor did she.

Then Jason said, 'You still haven't said—will you stay?'

'Yes.' Morgan's voice shook.

Something indefinable came and went in Jason's eyes at the word. Urgently Morgan searched his face but his expression, after that one second, became impersonal.

Morgan tried to ignore a feeling of disappointment. 'I guess I should get to the cookhouse, otherwise the men will go hungry. I can unpack later.'

She was about to walk past Jason when he stopped her. A finger touched her lips. 'A bruise, Morgan.'

A shiver went up her spine. 'Yes.'

'I have bruises too. Bigger ones, and turning blue. Only they're where you can't see them.'

Morgan laughed a little ruefully. 'I hope you're not asking for an apology?'

'No. You asked me to let you go and I didn't, so I guess I got what I deserved.' Unexpectedly his lips tilted in a wicked grin. 'You're a feisty lady, Morgan Muir. A bit of a spitfire.'

All at once her heart was racing. 'Jason... What the men told you was true. I didn't mean them to see the photos. I would never be so stupid as to tease them. Or so cruel. You needn't have been so angry.'

A brooding gaze swept over her, taking in every detail of her face: the eyes that expressed such a range of emotions; the lips that tasted so sweet; the throat where the pulse sometimes beat an exciting tattoo; the swell of her breasts beneath her T-shirt.

Jason knew very well why he had been so angry yesterday. There was far more to it than the sight of Hank, lustfully plastering his greasy mouth to Morgan's pictures—though that had been bad enough. There was the thought of the other cowboys, seeing Morgan in her semi-nude state. And that man—Damian—with his arms wrapped around her, his fingers touching her breasts. Jason could not *bear* the thought of other men seeing Morgan's lovely body and touching it. *Only me*, he thought, *only me*. The knowledge that he was jealous made him angrier still.

Suddenly he was moving towards her. It was as if a force stronger than himself was propelling him forwards—a force that was not part of his brain but something more elemental, involving his deepest emotions.

He didn't speak as he drew Morgan into his arms. For

a long moment they stood close together. Jason felt
Morgan, slim and soft in his arms, tremble just a little.
Her hair had a lovely smell, and he pressed his mouth
against it. The moment was so sweet that he was in no
hurry to end it.

It was only when Morgan drew back and looked up
at him that some sense of sanity returned, and with it
the knowledge that Morgan would not be at Six-Gate
Corral much longer—that she was a city girl who could
never be permanently happy on a ranch.

'I'm sorry,' he said once more, abruptly. And then he
turned and left the room.

Two days later, Jason said, 'I'm going to Austin tomorrow. Want to come along?'

Morgan looked at him in surprise. 'The last question
I expected.'

'Really?'

'You've been avoiding me, Jason, ever since you told
me to stay. Eating breakfast before I get back from the
cookhouse. Excuses not to have dinner with me as well.
If we've exchanged twenty words in two days it's been
a lot.'

'You've been counting, Morgan?'

Her head lifted at the challenge. 'Hasn't taken any
mathematical talent to do that. Still bothered about
Hank, Jason?'

'I thought we'd finished with that.'

'I thought so too. I hoped it was all done with, but it
seems I was wrong. Hank is gone, and you can't forgive
me.'

Wrong, Morgan, wrong. It's myself I can't forgive.

'I'm asking you to come to Austin with me,' he said
slowly. 'Doesn't that tell you something?'

'*Have* you forgiven me?'

A long moment passed. Then Jason said, 'There was nothing *to* forgive.'

A trembling began deep inside Morgan, and to hide it she asked, 'Why are you going to Austin?'

'Business to see to. Brent comes with me sometimes. Gives him a chance to stock up on the kind of things we can't purchase locally.'

'I see…'

'We'd go our separate ways and then meet for a meal, before heading back to the ranch.'

As always Morgan's treacherous heart leaped at the thought of spending time alone with Jason.

'Might be a nice idea,' she said brightly.

'That's settled, then. We'll leave some time after breakfast and be back at the ranch in time for supper.'

Morgan did a quick mental calculation, and frowned. 'Won't we have to leave a lot earlier if you have business to do and still want to drive all the way there and back in a day?'

Jason looked amused. 'Who said anything about driving? We'll fly, of course.'

'*Fly?*'

'You seem surprised. Surely you've seen the hangar, the plane and the runway.'

Morgan looked thoughtful. 'The hangar's been closed whenever I passed it. I didn't realize that it housed a plane in use.'

'It's the way we do things in Texas, Morgan. The distances are so vast here. From ranch to city. From one ranch to another—from one part of the state to another. Flying is the obvious mode of transport. Your grandfather must have told you that.'

'My grandfather was a cowboy, not a rancher or a pilot,' Morgan said drily. 'Bus, train or horse was his way of getting around. Who flies the plane, Jason?'

'I do.' He was laughing now. 'I wish you could see

yourself, Morgan. Your eyes are so wide and your expression so astonished.'

'I never realized that you were a pilot.'

'And now that you do know, does it change the way you feel about the trip?'

She did not have to think about the answer. 'No.'

'Sure, Morgan?'

She forced herself to remain still as Jason caught her chin in one of his big hands. 'Quite sure.'

'Good.'

'After all…' she grinned at him '…a whole day without any meals for me to cook—isn't that a cause for celebration?'

His eyes glittered. 'Is that the only thing on your mind?'

'Let's say it's one thing.'

'Meaning that you hate your daily stints in the cookhouse?'

'I don't hate them—in fact, I enjoy them more than I ever imagined I would—but I'm not averse to a holiday. By the way, what will the cowboys do about meals tomorrow, Jason?'

'You've seen the contingency food Brent keeps in the freezer. The men won't starve.'

'I'm glad.'

He brushed her throat with his thumb. 'Trust me to fly you safely, Morgan?'

Morgan tried to ignore the wicked thumb as it moved again. Jason's question was easy to answer: she had known some time ago that she would trust this man with her life.

'I do trust you,' she said simply.

An unreadable emotion moved in Jason's eyes. 'Tomorrow morning,' he said.

CHAPTER EIGHT

'NERVOUS, Morgan?'

Morgan had been sitting forward in her seat, gazing down over the brushland.

'Nervous?' Her eyes shone as she looked at Jason. 'Oh, no! Not at all! It all looks so different from the air, doesn't it, Jason? The colour of the brush. That huge herd of cattle down there to the right just a mass of tiny moving brown dots. And the ranch—I knew it was big, but from here it looks endless.'

Jason laughed. 'You're not seeing the half of it.'

'Maybe not. But it's awesome! Wonderful! The sense of freedom you get from up here, the vastness. Jason, you're laughing at me!'

He grinned. 'With you, not at you. You're so eager, Morgan, it's refreshing. You make me feel things I haven't thought about in years. But, Morgan, this can't be the first time you've flown.'

'Of course not. But sitting on a crowded plane is nothing like this. One of two hundred passengers. Your only contact with the pilot is a faceless voice over an intercom, wishing you a pleasant flight and asking you to fly with the airline again. This...' she made a wide gesture '...is so different.'

The biggest difference, of course, was the pilot at her side. Powerful, confident and totally in command of his plane. His very confidence was sexy.

'Did Vera fly with you often?'

'Why do you ask?'

'Just wondered,' she said, as lightly as she could. She wouldn't tell him that the experience was so special that she couldn't bear to think of him sharing it with some other woman.

'Vera likes luxury,' Jason said shortly. 'That includes having a solicitous flight attendant on hand to see to her every need. Besides, Vera loathed this little plane. She never felt safe in it.'

'She didn't know what she was missing.'

They landed in Austin—as smooth a landing as Morgan had ever known—and took a cab downtown. Jason told Morgan where they would meet for an early supper, and then they parted ways.

Morgan had been to Austin only once—when she and Brent had met to talk about the job—and for a while she wandered around, enjoying the sights and sounds of the pretty Texas city with its lovely views over the Colorado River.

Early in the afternoon she made a few purchases for the cookhouse. And then it was time to meet Jason at the restaurant.

He was there before her, and had already arranged for them to be seated at the best table. 'You must be starving,' he said when he saw her. 'Let's enjoy our meal, Morgan.'

Enjoy it they did. The food was delicious, and they got on as well as the previous time they had dined together. It was as if the disaster with the catalogue and with Hank had been wiped from both their minds.

When they left the restaurant they were amazed to find that the weather had changed: it was pouring. A pelting wind-driven rain lashed the streets and the pavements with all the power of a tropical storm. Lightning rent the sky and thunder roared.

'Pretty fierce,' Jason commented.

'Did you know it would rain?'

'Lord, no. I listened to the weather forecast several times yesterday and again early this morning before leaving the ranch, but there was nothing to indicate a storm. If I'd known this was brewing we wouldn't have flown.'

'It's really something.' Morgan stepped backwards as lightning lit the storm-darkened street.

'Happens sometimes,' Jason said. 'A storm right out of nowhere. Taking all the weathermen by surprise— playing games with their predictions.'

'What will we do, Jason?'

'We definitely can't fly back to the ranch tonight. Not unless it clears quickly, and at this point there's not much chance of that. We'll have to stay the night in Austin, Morgan. I have a condo we can go to.' He flashed her a quick, searching look. 'Two bedrooms. But perhaps you'd prefer to check into a hotel?'

'The condo will be fine,' Morgan said over the sudden rapid beating of her heart. She could have told Jason that even had there been only one room she would not have minded. Would have preferred it, if the truth be told.

I've become shameless. Who would have thought it possible that I could change so much in so short a time?

It was not easy to hail a cab—it was as if the whole city had been caught off guard by the downpour—but Jason managed to stop one.

The condominium building was set a little way back from the road, with a garden in front of it. They had to run from the pavement along a path to the lobby, and by the time they got inside they were both soaked.

In the hallway of Jason's condo they stopped and looked at each other. Water dripped from their hair, their necks, their hands and their clothes, making big puddles on the tiled floor.

At the same moment they burst out laughing.

'Talk about drowned rats,' Morgan gasped when she

could talk, and for some reason the comment made them laugh even harder.

'You don't mind, Morgan?' Jason asked when their laughter had subsided.

'Should I?'

'Your clothes are soaking and your hair's a mess.'

'My hair isn't a problem, and my clothes will dry,' Morgan said cheerfully.

'They won't dry at all if you don't get them off.'

She shot him a dancing look. 'You want me to take off my clothes?'

'I want a lot more than that,' Jason said gruffly.

He put out his arms to her, and she went into them willingly. For a long moment they stood together, two wet bodies in dripping clothes. It was a moment so exciting that Morgan felt as if her heart might beat a pathway right through the wall of her chest.

And then Jason loosened his arms and looked down at her. 'Morgan…'

'Yes?' The mischief left her eyes as she tilted her head back.

'You are so lovely. So incredibly sexy. You do know that I want to kiss you?'

'Yes,' she whispered.

God, the way she was looking at him—the melting expression in her eyes, the softly parted lips, the rise and fall of her breasts beneath the wet blouse.

'There are two rooms, Morgan—what if we pretended that there was only one?'

'Why don't we?' The words came out in a whisper. Morgan's cheeks were flushed, her eyes luminous.

'Do you mean that?' Jason asked raggedly.

'Oh, yes.'

'You're not teasing, Morgan?'

'I wouldn't tease about a thing like that,' she said unsteadily.

'Morgan! Beautiful Morgan!'

He drew her against him once more, a little roughly this time, passion in every inch—every muscle—of his long body. Morgan could barely breathe. She knew what was about to happen, and she wanted it more than she had ever wanted anything. The fact that she would be making love with a man for the first time in her life did not frighten her at all.

'Morgan.' Jason's lips moved in her wet hair. And then he was loosening his arms once more. 'I've been waiting for this for so long.'

Love and need and passion took away Morgan's shyness and inhibitions so that she was able to say what was on her mind. At this moment there could be no barriers between herself and the man she loved. Giving herself no time to regret the words, she said, 'I've waited too, Jason.'

She was awed when she felt him shudder. That she had the power to move a man as tough as Jason seemed incredible. Her chest was full, and in her throat a lump was forming. She loved this man. She had never imagined that she could love anyone so deeply.

With the tips of her fingers she traced a light pathway around his lips. 'About the room, Jason,' she whispered. 'We could pretend all night.'

He gave another shudder, even stronger this time. When Jason spoke his voice was more ragged than before. 'As long as you know what you're getting into.'

'I do.' She stopped herself from adding the words, 'my love'.

'No stopping, Morgan.'

'None,' she promised as steadily as she could. Beneath her fingertips Jason's lips quivered.

'You are so beautiful, Morgan, so sexy. You drive me out of my mind with wanting you.'

Then he was kissing her deeply, passionately, yet with

all the tenderness that was in him—a tenderness that had been too long suppressed. Morgan's hands went around his neck and she was kissing him too, telling him with her lips of the feelings and emotions she had never been able to put into words.

Her ardour must have excited Jason. As he took breath Morgan heard a rough groan. And then he was kissing her again, with such urgency that small moans of pleasure escaped Morgan's lips. Overcome by a longing that was stronger than anything she had ever known, she arched against him. And that brought another groan from his throat.

'Two reasons now to get out of our clothes,' Jason said at length. 'Our things can dry while we make love.'

Morgan laughed softly. 'What an excuse to undress.'

He was laughing too. Then he said, 'Will you let me undress you, sweetheart?'

Sweetheart… It was the first time Jason had used the endearment. Morgan felt as if she might burst with happiness.

She was shy as Jason began to unbutton her blouse, but she didn't move away from him or suggest that she undress herself. One button, then another came free, not sliding as easily as usual through the wet fabric.

'All done,' Jason said at last. 'And now I need to kiss you again.…'

His lips brushed her throat, evoking a sensation so erotic that Morgan gasped and closed her eyes. And then his lips went lower, to her breasts—a tantalising caress that set her nerves screaming. Every inch of her body was on fire now and all rational thought left her. She was just a mass of raw sensation and craving.

A door opened somewhere, then closed. Distantly Morgan heard the sound, but thought nothing of it. Her mind was solely on their love-making. Soon…soon they would be together in the way she'd dreamed about for so long.

'Jason?' someone said.

For a moment neither Morgan nor Jason reacted.

'*Jason*!'

Abruptly Jason's lips jerked from Morgan's breasts. Their heads turned at the same moment in the direction of the voice. And then they froze.

A woman had appeared in the condominium. A very beautiful woman, Morgan registered a little numbly. Her hair and her make-up were flawless, barely even wet. Without speaking, she gave her huge umbrella a shake before she put it on the floor. Then she said, 'Well.' Just the one word.

'Vera!' Jason exclaimed.

'Well, and don't you both look surprised.' Hard eyes flicked across them disdainfully, her gaze going from Morgan to Jason before coming to rest on Morgan. 'Never expected to be caught in the act, I guess.'

As the woman continued to look at her a deep flush stained Morgan's cheeks. A minute earlier she had been so happy and now she felt cheap and exposed.

'What are you doing here?' Jason demanded.

'Same as you, darling. Well, not quite the same.' An amused look was on her face. 'All *I* was after was shelter from the rain, whereas you obviously have other things on your mind.'

'How did you get in?'

'With my key.'

'I thought you gave it back when we parted.'

'No. You didn't notice, and I decided to hold onto it. I come here quite often, Jason. It's useful, this place. Of course it's too bad for you that I'm here today. Guess you thought you'd enjoy a bit of private entertainment, before heading back to the ranch.'

'This isn't what you think,' Jason said harshly.

'Are you kidding?' Vera laughed, a loud, unpleasant sound. 'You always liked your sex, didn't you, Jason, darling? And men of your type—cowboys—like common women. Like this one.'

'That's enough, Vera.'

'Oh, come, darling, from what I saw it's clear what you were up to so why pretend otherwise? We're all adults, aren't we? You, me and the bimbo.'

A furious Morgan was about to speak when Jason said harshly, 'Don't you dare call her that!'

'Heavens, you really are touchy. Look, Jason, it's just as well you're here. You know I've been wanting to talk to you.'

'This isn't the time, Vera.'

'The bimbo won't mind waiting a few minutes.' Vera turned to Morgan. 'Will you?'

Morgan's cheeks had grown even hotter. Her fingernails dug painfully into her palms, but she didn't dignify Vera with an answer. Looking at Jason, she said quietly, 'I'll go to one of the bedrooms while the two of you talk. I should be getting out of the rest of these wet clothes anyway.'

'This won't take long, Morgan,' he said tightly.

'*Morgan*!' Vera exclaimed, looking astonished. 'Your name is Morgan?'

Morgan turned from the door. 'What difference does my name make? We've never met.'

Vera rounded on Jason. 'You were talking to a Morgan the last time I phoned. I remember the name because I thought at first you were talking to a man. How long have you and the bimbo been together?'

'I am not a bimbo,' Morgan said clearly. 'Stop calling me that.'

'I call a spade a spade—and don't tell me about clichés.' Vera's tone was vicious. 'My ex-husband likes women. Do you know what this place is? A love-nest for his bimbos. You're not the first, lady, and you won't be the last.'

'How dare you, Vera!' Jason's face had become a tight mask of anger.

'Do you deny it darling?' Vera taunted. 'Well, do you?'

'I don't owe you any answers, Vera.' He turned his head as Morgan made for one of the bedroom doors. 'Where are you going?'

'Leaving the two of you to talk alone.' Morgan's deliberately quiet tone hid her tension.

'Whatever it is that Vera has to say she can say it in front of you,' Jason said harshly.

'You surprise me, darling. Have your bimbos become privy to your personal conversations?' Vera's eyes sparkled with venom.

'You don't seem to have heard me,' Morgan told her. 'I am not a bimbo.'

'C'mon, a girl who amuses Jason at the ranch and here at the condo? This may be the nineties but some things don't change.'

'If you call her a bimbo again I won't answer for the consequences,' Jason warned.

'In any case, you're quite wrong about me,' Morgan put in. 'I happen to have a job at the ranch.'

'You don't have to explain yourself to my ex-wife,' Jason said.

He was right about that, Morgan thought, yet she didn't like the conclusions Vera was drawing. She felt the need to give the woman the basic facts.

'What kind of work?' Vera looked suspicious. 'Don't tell me you've taken to employing cowgirls, Jason?'

'I'm the ranch cook,' Morgan informed her.

'What happened to Brent?'

'He's gone away for a month. I'm working in his place.'

Vera looked unconvinced. 'When does he get back?'

'It shouldn't concern you, but a week from Friday.' There was such an odd note in Jason's tone. Morgan didn't know what to make of it.

'Well, isn't that something, darling?' Vera's laughter was openly contemptuous. 'Brent takes a vacation and you get yourself a cook *and* a playmate. That's really quite funny.'

'Get out, Vera.' Jason's tone held a warning. Anyone else would have heeded it and retreated.

Not Vera. 'We need to talk, darling.'

'No.'

But Jason's ex-wife was persistent. 'It's as good a time as any. You're here, I'm here. Whatever the two of you were up to can wait surely, darling?'

Darling... With what ease the endearment rolled off Vera's tongue. As easily as the word 'bimbo.' Morgan wished that Vera would go. In her presence she felt uncomfortable and dishevelled.

Jason advanced on Vera. 'How many more times do I have to ask you to leave?'

Vera eyed him, uncertain for the first time. 'It's pouring out there, Jason.'

'You didn't get too wet on your way in—your umbrella's the size of a house. You've always been able to take care of yourself.'

In a second the expression in Vera's eyes changed, the uncertainty replaced by a glinting triumph. 'So that's what this is all about. You're still hurting, Jason. You've never got over the fact that I left you.'

'Go, Vera.'

'Oh, I'll go. But don't think you've seen the last of me, Jason. We'll still have that talk. I know you'll find it *very* interesting.' She shot a poisonous glance at Morgan. 'As for you, bimbo, enjoy him while you can.'

'The key, Vera.' Jason held out his hand as she walked to the door.

She looked startled. 'You're asking me to give you my key?'

'*My* key, if you remember.'

Vera's cheeks reddened. 'I won't give it to you.'

'Very well,' Jason said pleasantly. 'Keep it if you wish. It's not worth an argument. But don't bother coming here again. If you do you'll find that the locks have been changed.'

From across the room Morgan heard the furious hissing intake of Vera's breath. Vera looked from Jason to Morgan, and Morgan was shocked to see the hatred in the other woman's eyes.

Half a minute went by. Then Vera's expression changed once again as she gave Jason the key. 'I understand that I barged in here at the wrong time so I'll go. Never let it be said that I stood in the way of your having a good time, Jason. But we will have that talk—soon.'

Jason followed her to the door. When she had gone he put the chain into the slot. He was taking no chance on the possibility that Vera might take it into her head to come back.

With the door secured, he turned. 'Morgan…' he said, and stopped. The room was empty.

He found her in one of the bedrooms, trying to straighten her wet clothing.

'Morgan—what are you doing?' he asked.

She didn't turn her head, but Jason saw the tightness in the slender neck and shoulders.

'What does it look like?' she responded when she had finished buttoning her wet blouse.

'You can't be thinking of going?'

'I am.'

Jason tensed. 'It's still pouring. Besides, where would you go? I have no intention of flying in this weather, and the plane is your only way back to the ranch to-night.'

Morgan didn't answer immediately. Jason ached to take her in his arms, but her rigid posture made him realize that she might not welcome the embrace.

Her face was a little pale as she turned to him. 'I can find a hotel.'

'You could—but why would you want to?'

'Isn't it obvious, Jason?'

He did try to put his arms around her then, but she pushed her hands against his chest. 'Don't!'

Jason dropped his arms. 'What's got into you, Morgan?' he asked roughly.

'I think you know.' Disappointment clogged her voice.

'You were fine until Vera arrived. We were going to make love, Morgan.'

'That's right. Me—and all those others.'

'Which others?' Jason's face had gone cold and hard with contempt.

'The other women in your life. You were going to make love to me in…in this love-nest.' Her voice shook.

'Are you telling me that you believe Vera?'

She made herself meet his eyes. 'You didn't deny it.'

'Damn right I didn't.'

'Why not, Jason? How did you think I felt? Standing there half-naked, listening to the terrible things Vera said. If they weren't true surely you'd have denied them.'

'I didn't feel I had to defend myself.' His voice was flat.

'I wonder why not.'

As if the physical contact repelled him, Jason dropped Morgan's wrist. 'In other words, you do believe Vera?'

'I don't know what to believe.' Morgan fought back the tears that welled in her eyes.

But Jason refused to help her. 'You're an adult, Morgan. If you don't know what to believe I can't do anything about it.' His voice had turned to ice. 'So where does that leave us?'

Us… The word that should have had such wonderful connotations meant nothing now. Morgan could not bear to look at Jason, who was as harshly aloof and hostile as the first time she had met him.

'If…if I stay here I'll sleep in this room,' she told him unsteadily. 'You can spend the night in the other one.'

Jason's eyes took on a hooded look, making them impossible to read. 'You do realize—' his tone was measured '—that if Vera hadn't disturbed us we would even now be making love?'

Morgan's lips quivered. 'Maybe I should be thankful to her for walking in when she did.'

'If you believe that then there's nothing more to be said.' Jason was at the door when he stopped and looked at her. 'You do understand that it's up to you now, don't you?'

Something in his tone turned the blood in her veins to ice. 'What do you mean, Jason?'

'You have to make your own choices. Do you believe me or do you believe Vera? Do you want to make love? If you do, you know where to find me. I'll be in the other bedroom. If not, that's fine too—I won't try to convince you any further.'

Anger, hot and wild, coursed through her at his arrogance. 'You have some nerve, Jason. Asking me who I believe when you've given me no facts. All I have to go on is what Vera said.'

'If you expect me to give you facts you're wasting your time.' His jaw was firm, his mouth a hard line. 'I repeat, Morgan, whatever happens now is up to you.'

He was walking through the door when she took a step towards him. 'Jason…'

But if he heard her he didn't turn back, and Morgan didn't call his name again. She stood quite still as the door closed behind him. To her horror, an angry sob rose in her throat but she managed to stifle it. She couldn't let Jason hear her cry.

Making her way to the window, she pressed her face against the pane. It was still raining. Looking down at the sodden trees outside the building—at the cars moving more slowly than usual—Morgan shivered. Her momentary anger was gone and now she felt cold.

Jason would not be back, she was certain of that. There had been finality in his words and his tone. It was safe to take off her wet clothes and crawl into bed.

Time passed. The door of the second bedroom opened, then closed. Outside it grew dark. Eventually the rain stopped, but Morgan's coldness remained. Even without her wet clothes, lying beneath the blanket, she still felt cold.

Jason's words sounded in her mind—echoing, reverberating, refusing to be silenced. 'If Vera hadn't disturbed us we would even now be making love.' And, 'It's up to you now...'

Who should she believe—Jason or Vera? That awful, hard-faced woman? Or the man who had made a permanent place for himself in Morgan's heart?

She wanted so much to believe Jason. At the same time the thought that she was just one of a procession of women made her feel sick. If Jason were to give a sign that he loved her, everything would be so different. As it was, she didn't even know whether he liked her very much.

But if she didn't believe Jason then that meant believing Vera, a woman who spat out venom with every word she spoke.

Jason or Vera? Vera or Jason? The answer came to her some time during the night.

*   *   *

'Morgan?' Jason asked. He was lying on the bed.

Morgan couldn't tell from his voice whether he was surprised to see her or not. She licked dry lips. 'Yes…'

'What are you doing here?'

'You said…' Her voice shook. 'You said it was up to me…'

'Yes?'

'Whether we…'

'Whether we?' he prompted softly.

Why was he making it so difficult for her? Bravely she said, 'Whether we make love.'

He was still on the bed. 'Is that what you want, Morgan?'

After a long moment she whispered, 'Yes.' The word was torn from a parched throat.

'What made you change your mind?'

This wasn't going at all the way she had imagined it—Jason pulling her into his arms, telling her he was sorry they had argued and covering her with a thousand kisses. Instead, he was asking her all these questions.

'What made you change your mind?' he asked again.

'It doesn't matter,' she said dully.

'It does to me.' There was a strange urgency in his tone.

The curtains were open and a streetlight cast a glow through the window, making it possible to see the outline of the man on the bed, his legs crossed at the ankles and hands clasped behind his head. It wasn't, however, light enough to make out his expression.

'I…I realized you were right about one thing,' Morgan said at length. 'If Vera hadn't come when she did we would have been making love. And I…I wouldn't have known anything about…about a love-nest.' The last words were an effort.

'Did you believe her, Morgan?'

She hesitated. 'We've been over that.'

'*Did* you believe her?'

'Does that matter too?'

'Even more than the last question.' That same strange urgency was still in his voice.

Morgan knew what Jason wanted to hear. She had spent hours agonizing over this very question. And in the end the answer was really quite simple.

'I might have believed her then. I don't any more.'

'No love-nest?'

'No.'

What Morgan could have said was that it didn't matter. So deeply in love was she that she was willing to ignore Jason's past.

'Does that mean that you trust me over Vera?' Again she noticed the odd tone.

Over anyone. And with her life.

'Yes,' she said.

There was silence. An intense silence so highly charged that Morgan felt as if she could reach out and touch the sparks in the air between Jason and herself. Acutely conscious all at once of her semi-naked state—all she had on was bra and panties—her hands went up to cover her breasts.

At that same moment Jason swung his legs over the side of the bed.

'Come here, Morgan.'

'Jason…'

'I want to look at you.'

'Jason…' she said again. Now that the moment had arrived she felt suddenly nervous.

He came towards her, a superb figure lit by the glow of the streetlight and wearing only a pair of brief shorts. No other man could compare with him, Morgan thought.

'Sweetheart,' he said raggedly. Putting his hands over hers, he took them from her breasts. Then he took a step back and looked at her.

Beneath his gaze Morgan felt a burning heat spreading through her. Her shyness faded so that she was able to stand quite still as his eyes went over her—from her throat down to her breasts and waist and over her hips and thighs. Sensing Jason's throbbing excitement, she was elated once more that she was able to make him feel this way.

'Morgan…' His tone was rough, a little broken. 'So beautiful. So incredibly lovely. Oh, Morgan, sweetheart, I want you so much.'

A second later his arms were around her. As if they were deliberately holding back, they began to touch each other's faces, mouths, lips and pathways around eyes—pathways of exploration, preludes to passion. And then Jason was kissing Morgan hungrily, as if he could never get enough of her.

And she was kissing him too, roused to fever pitch by the heat of the almost naked body against her own—by the lips and tongue exploring her mouth, the hands moving over her and by her passionate love for him. She was also kissing him and exploring him with her hands, making love to him as he was to her.

By the time Jason lifted her in his arms and carried her to the bed every part of Morgan was clamouring for the fulfilment that only this man could give her.

He lay down beside her and gathered her in his arms. They began to kiss once more, caressing and exploring each other—hip against hip, thigh against thigh, arms and legs entwined—their hearts beating in frenzied unison as they raised each other to ever-greater heights of excitement. This was the love-making of which she had so often dreamed.

It was only when the long body settled over hers that Morgan remembered the one thing that he didn't know about her.

'Jason…'

His lips were so close to hers that when he replied his breath filled her mouth. 'We can't stop now, Morgan.'

Stop? She could no more stop what was happening than she could stop the next beat of her heart.

'Jason... You have to know... I'm a virgin.'

'A *virgin*!' The word exploded from him. So many things he had thought about this girl, but never this. Never once this!

There was another charged silence. 'You're disappointed,' Morgan whispered at last.

'*Disappointed*? Amazed is more like it. Stunned! I never thought, never dreamed that you hadn't... And so *glad*, Morgan, so glad I'm the first.' He raised his head and looked down at her. In a new tone he asked, 'Are you sure you want this?'

'As sure as I've ever been about anything.' The words came out on a shuddering breath. 'Jason... Is there something we should...?' She didn't finish the sentence.

But Jason seemed to understand. He left the bed, returning to her quickly. 'You'll be protected, Morgan. No need for you to worry about that.'

Once more his body covered hers, heating it and raising her to fever pitch—sending passion and desire coursing through every part of her being.

The moment came when Morgan felt that she couldn't wait another second and, miraculously, Jason seemed to know it. The brief moment of pain when he entered her was replaced by an ecstasy unlike anything she had ever imagined. An ecstasy that drew shudders from her body and cries of pleasure from her lips. And suddenly it was as if something were exploding inside her—something fierce and savage, glorious and wonderful. She didn't know that she was calling his name. 'Jason! *Oh, Jason!*'

Afterwards they lay together a long time, kissing, caressing and talking softly. Almost at the same moment they became aroused again, and they made love once more—not with quite the frenzy of the first time but with just as much satisfaction and joy.

CHAPTER NINE

THERE were times in the next week when Morgan thought that she was floating, her feet never seeming to be less than six inches above the ground. Since the night in Austin there had been a dramatic change in her relationship with Jason. There was always something to talk about and to laugh about, and mealtimes were animated in a way they had never been before. Afterwards they would listen to music and sometimes they danced, with Morgan showing the tall cowboy steps that he had never tried before but which he learned with amazing speed.

Best of all was their love-making. When the curtains had been drawn against the darkness they would kiss and caress, and each time they made love was as exciting as the first time.

In her spare time Morgan began to add softening touches to the ranch-house—vases of flowers to brighten the spartan rooms, and posters which she found in the nearby town to adorn some of the walls. There was much more she would have liked to have done in the way of decoration but she was hesitant about overstepping the limits of her relationship with Jason, a man who never once mentioned a shared future. To her surprise, though, he didn't seem to object to her efforts. If anything, he seemed to welcome them.

Morgan was about to leave the cookhouse one evening when Charlie stopped her.

'I've met a girl,' he said.

'Charlie, that's great!'

'Her name is Sally.' His eyes glowed.

'How did you two meet?'

In a diner frequented by the cowboys, he told her. Sally was a waitress, and new in town. They had got talking, one thing had led to another and now he was hoping to see Sally regularly.

He took a photo from his pocket. The two of them were standing together, the big cowboy with his arm around a red-haired girl with a pretty face and an attractive open smile.

'I'm hoping she'll marry me,' Charlie said.

'Oh, I hope so too, Charlie. Sally couldn't have found a nicer guy. Where will you live?'

'Jason will give us a place.' He smiled shyly. 'The two of you could be friends, Morgan.'

They could indeed. Morgan could tell, just from the photo, that she would get on well with Sally. Only one little detail stood in the way of friendship.

'I won't be here,' she said. 'Brent will be back in a couple of days, and I'll be leaving the ranch then.'

Charlie's mouth opened; it wasn't hard to guess what he was going to say. But he thought better of it, and Morgan was glad. It would have been very difficult for her to hear the words, and harder still to tell him why there was little possibility of a future for Jason and herself.

She watched Charlie leave the cookhouse, happy that the gentle cowboy, who would make a wonderful husband, had found someone to love. She couldn't help envying Sally. Charlie was prepared for commitment. If only the same were true of Jason.

On Thursday Morgan said, 'Brent will be back tomorrow.'

'Sure will.' Jason's eyes sparkled in a grin. 'Glad the month is over, Morgan?'

Glad? 'Looks as if *you* are glad,' she said over the pain that tore like a twisting knife-blade at her heart.

Jason's grin deepened wickedly. He made no attempt

to deny her words, and when he walked away from her
in the direction of the stables he was whistling.

Morgan watched him numbly. Whistling! And that in-
furiating grin. Rarely had she seen Jason in such a good
mood. It could only mean one thing—he was pleased
that Brent was coming back to the ranch and that she
was leaving.

'I'll pack after breakfast,' she told him on her way to
the cookhouse the next morning.

'Hold the packing.'

Her eyes searched his face. 'I don't understand.'

'Brent won't be here.'

Briefly hope stirred. '*Ever*?'

'Not today. He called a few minutes ago. Seems he
sprained his ankle—a cowboy, can you imagine? Anyway, he won't be back for another two days.'

Two more days at the ranch. It was foolish to be so
happy because the extra time would make no difference
in the end.

'Sunday, then,' Morgan said slowly.

'Oh, yes, Morgan, Sunday.'

Again she saw that wicked grin. Morgan felt like
throttling Jason.

The next day a car stopped on the driveway, and the
front door of the house was flung open before Morgan
could open it. She took a step backwards, as surprised
to see Vera as that woman was to see her.

Vera was the first to speak. 'What the hell are you
doing here?' she demanded.

Morgan clenched her hands and counted to ten. When
she could trust herself to speak calmly she said, 'I work
here—remember?'

'Only till yesterday. Till the end of Brent's vacation.
You should have left by now.'

'You seem,' Morgan said pleasantly, 'put out that I'm still here.'

'*Put out*?'

'Yes. Why is that?'

The other woman's face took on an angry flush. 'Not yours to ask, bimbo.'

'I thought we'd agreed you weren't going to call me that.'

'We didn't agree, and I'll call you anything I like. If I'm put out it's only because I thought I'd wait till you were gone before coming here. You haven't answered my question—why are you still at the ranch?'

'Not that it's any of your business…' Morgan lifted her chin '…but Brent was detained.'

'He is coming, though?'

'Of course.'

'Well.' The other woman's face brightened instantly. 'Where is Jason? Out on the range?'

Morgan nodded.

Vera was regarding her thoughtfully. 'I came here to talk to him—as I said, I thought you'd be gone by now—but you and I may as well have a talk too.'

'I very much doubt,' Morgan said tightly, 'that we have anything to talk about.'

She was walking away when Vera caught her arm. 'There are things you should know, *bimbo*—just in case you have any thoughts of staying on at the ranch after Brent gets back. And don't give me that affronted look. I know what I saw that day in the condo. The way you were cosying up to my husband was revolting. You may be the ranch cook, but the two of you weren't discussing recipes.'

'Jason isn't your husband,' Morgan said.

'He was. He will be again.' Vera's eyes glittered. '*That's* what Jason and I are going to talk about—right after he gets in.'

Morgan's throat had gone so dry that it hurt her to swallow. 'You were divorced. What makes you think that Jason wants to get together with you again?'

'I know he does. It's all been one big misunderstanding.'

'You walked out on Jason.'

'He told you that, did he?' Vera's lips twisted unpleasantly. 'Nothing like an injured husband to gain the attentions of a willing woman. Not that I can complain about that, I guess. Jason is all man, and if the temporary cook is willing to let him have some easy sex why shouldn't he take it? The fact is, Morgan—that is your name, isn't it? The fact is that my husband won't be needing another woman's attentions when I move back to the ranch.'

'You seem very certain of yourself,' Morgan said in a low voice.

'With reason. Poor, darling Jason, I hurt him so badly. Did he tell you that too? He was terribly upset when I left him—tried so hard to convince me to stay. He'll be over the moon with happiness when he hears I'm coming back.'

It was true that Jason had been hurt—he had said so more than once. So maybe, Morgan thought painfully, he would really be happy at the thought of Vera's return.

Pointedly she looked at Vera's hand on her arm. 'I have things to do.'

'In a moment. I haven't heard you say you'll be off the moment Brent gets back.'

When Morgan remained silent the fingers on her arm tightened, the long nails biting into her skin. Suddenly she was very angry. 'I don't have to tell you anything, Vera.'

'*Mrs Delaney* to you. So you are planning to ensnare my husband?'

'My plans don't concern you.'

The nails bit deeper. 'Damn you, bimbo! You'll leave

when Brent comes. Do you understand? I'll be mistress here, and I'll give the orders. In fact, why don't you leave right now? I'll explain to Jason.'

'That won't be necessary.' Morgan jerked her arm out of Vera's grip.

She was in the kitchen, furiously rolling out pastry, when the man himself came through the back door.

'Wondered if I'd find you here,' he said, and held out his arms to her.

Morgan ignored the invitation. 'Hello.'

'Anything wrong?' Jason asked, as he took the roll-ing-pin out of her hands and drew her against him. 'Something tells me you've had a tough day.'

Just for a moment Morgan gave in to her longings, closed her eyes and leaned against him. It wasn't Jason's fault that his ex-wife was a bitch.

'I'll have a wash, and then we can—' He broke off abruptly. In a new tone Jason exclaimed, '*Vera*!'

Morgan's eyes snapped open in time to see a furious Vera, glaring at them both. 'I thought I heard voices,' the woman said.

'What are you doing here, Vera?' Jason asked.

'Remember that talk we were going to have, darling?' With what seemed like a miraculous transformation of expression Vera threw Jason a brilliant smile. 'You do remember, don't you?'

Jason's arms loosened their hold. 'How could I for-get?' Moving away from Morgan, he said to Vera, 'OK, in my office. Let's get on with it.'

They were at the door of the kitchen when Vera stopped. 'Tell your cook to make us something to eat, will you, darling?'

'I don't think—' Jason began, but Vera interrupted him.

'I thought she'd have left the ranch by now—she tells me she's eager to be off the moment Brent gets back—but since she's still in your employ she may as well make herself useful. Sandwiches, Morgan, and a pot of strong coffee. No cream, no sugar.'

'Morgan,' said Jason, 'take no notice. This isn't part of your job.'

'I'll do it anyway,' Morgan told him grimly.

Twenty minutes later she took a tray to the ranch office. Vera and Jason were deep in conversation, but they stopped talking when she pushed open the door and carried the tray to the desk. Vera's face was flushed, but Morgan didn't notice that as she put down mugs, coffee-pot and a platter of sandwiches.

Jason stood up. 'Desk's a bit small for all these things you've brought, Morgan.' He glanced around him. 'I'd forgotten that table in the corner. I'll bring it over here.'

He was walking away from the two women when Vera moved. Lightning swift, she grabbed the coffee-pot. A blood-curdling scream emerged from her lips at the same time as a huge stain spread over her immaculate white pants.

The whole thing took no more than a few seconds, happening so quickly that Morgan was stunned. It was like some bizarre episode in a movie—inexplicable, unexpected—taking the viewer so completely by surprise that there was no time for thought or even for reaction. There was certainly no time to rationalize what had occurred.

The scream had Jason whirling around. 'Vera! What happened?'

'Burnt! She burned me! Morgan!' Vera spluttered the words.

In a second Jason was at Vera's side. 'Are you OK?'

'*No*! No, I'm not OK! Didn't you hear what I said? She burned me! Look!' Vera gestured frantically towards the stain. 'Coffee! Boiling hot! Oh, God, I'm probably scarred for life. She did it, Jason. The bimbo.'

'I didn't—' Morgan began.

But Vera interrupted. 'Deliberately, Jason! You should have seen her! The moment your back was turned! She just picked up the pot and poured it right over me. My God, Jason, we should call the police—have the bimbo charged!'

As she listened to Vera's wild accusations a great calm came over Morgan. She had tried once to defend herself but Vera had put a stop to that. She wouldn't try again. She shouldn't have to explain because that meant descending to Vera's level, and she refused to do that. Jason knew his ex-wife; he would see right through her despicable melodrama.

'Do something, Jason!' Vera's voice had risen, and she was rapidly becoming hysterical.

Jason turned to Morgan. 'You're very quiet.'

She gave him a level look. 'I'd have thought there was enough noise around here without adding to it.'

'Listen to her!' Vera screeched. 'The bimbo is brazen, on top of everything else.'

'Did you pour coffee over Vera's pants?' Jason asked.

In a second Morgan went rigid. Disbelievingly, she stared at Jason. Had he really asked the question?

'*Did* you?' he asked.

She found her voice. 'Why don't you tell me,' she said.

'Brazen,' Vera yelled. 'More than brazen.'

'Vera says you poured coffee over her pants.' Jason's tone had turned dangerously quiet. 'So far I've only heard her side of the story. Did you do it, Morgan?'

It took a great effort of will to stop her lips from quivering. 'I don't have to answer your questions, Jason.'

Jason was beginning to look exasperated. 'Don't you understand, Morgan? I'm giving you a chance to explain.'

'I understand,' she said hardily, 'that I don't have to

explain a thing. Not one thing, Jason. I'm not in the witness box.'

With that, Morgan pushed past Vera and Jason. As she made for the door she didn't stop to look at Vera's face. Had she done so, the woman's triumphant expression might have given her pause.

It didn't take Morgan long to throw her suitcase on her bed, and to fling in her few possessions and her clothes. She was at her car, with the door open, when Jason found her.

'Where do you think you're going?' he demanded.

'What does it look like? I'm leaving.' Giving him no chance to speak, she rushed on. 'You're rid of me, Jason. You're finally rid of me, just as you've wanted all along.'

'You can't just leave, Morgan.'

'Because you need me here one more day? To make supper tonight and breakfast in the morning? Sorry, Jason, but Brent will be back some time tomorrow and the men will have to make do until then. It's just as well Vera's here—she can help out.'

'Let me speak, Morgan—'

'What's the point? There's nothing left to say, Jason. Not any longer. I was dreading our parting tomorrow. I didn't know how I was going to say goodbye to you. In the end, I needn't have worried.'

A muscle moved at the top of his throat. 'What are you saying?'

'At least we've been spared a painful farewell. *I've* been spared—I don't think you care. Loving a man can be hell when he doesn't...'

Morgan stopped for just a second, aware that she was probably saying far more than she should. On the other hand, perhaps she hadn't said enough for there were things that she would never have a chance to say again.

Ignoring Jason's stunned expression, she rushed on.

'You don't deserve my love, Jason Delaney. You never did.'

'*Morgan!*'

'A man who would listen to Vera's vile accusations and believe them. Even if you wanted me—which you don't—you wouldn't deserve me. Goodbye, Jason.'

Jason had the look of a man in shock. His throat was corded, and beneath his tan he was suddenly ashen. Raggedly he said, 'Morgan, you can't—'

'I can do anything I want!' With that she leaped into the car, slammed the door shut and locked it.

Jason held onto the doorhandle as she turned the key and started the car. '*Morgan!* Don't be a fool, Morgan! We have to talk!'

'Vera's waiting for you,' she taunted as she released the brake. 'She has something very interesting to tell you, so why don't you talk to her instead? Go back to her, Jason. I'm sure you'll be pleased you did.'

The handle jerked out of Jason's fingers as Morgan put her foot on the accelerator and sped off.

As she drove away from the ranch-house Morgan was intent only on putting as many miles as she could between herself and the man she had loved. *Still loved.*

That was the awful thing—she still loved Jason. He had betrayed her. She ought to be able to stop loving him. But even in her state of grief and shock Morgan knew that wouldn't happen—not in a hurry, maybe never. It gave her no joy to know that she would always love Jason.

She was dry-eyed as she drove away from the house, too shocked to weep. The tears came only gradually, filling her eyes and choking her throat. On all sides was Six-Gate Corral land. Behind her, hidden in the cloud of dust stirred up by the car, was the ranch-house—and Jason, the most important person in her life.

Morgan had driven several miles when dimly, on the periphery of her mind, she became aware of a sound somewhere behind her but she paid it no attention. All she could think of was Jason, cold and grim-faced, demanding to know about the terrible thing she had done to poor Vera.

She started as a car shot past her. Was Vera leaving so soon?

But there was no time to dwell on Vera's unexpected departure because a minute later there was another sound. Three sharp honks on a car's horn. Looking in the mirror, Morgan saw a vehicle that she recognized. There was more honking, accompanied by a gesture of the driver's hand. Jason was telling Morgan to stop her car at the side of the road.

The utter nerve of the man! Well, he was dead wrong if he thought that he could order her around. They covered another mile, with Jason honking and Morgan ignoring him.

Suddenly Jason shot past her. When he stopped the vehicle in the middle of the road Morgan had no option but to slam on her brakes. In a moment he had leaped out of the Jeep and was running towards her.

'Are you crazy? We could have had an accident,' she yelled at him through her open window. 'Stopping like that two inches in front of me.'

'Don't exaggerate.' He was grinning. 'It wasn't two inches, and I knew exactly what I was doing. Besides, it looked as if you weren't going to stop.'

'That's right, I wasn't.'

'And I had no intention of following you all the way to Austin, or wherever it was you were planning to drive.'

'You didn't have to follow me anywhere, Jason.'

'Didn't I? Didn't I, Morgan?'

'No...' But her voice was quieter now.

Reaching through the window, Jason let a finger brush a path around her eyes. 'You've been crying.'

Morgan tried to turn away from him, but found that

she couldn't because her body betrayed her by refusing to move.

'Why?' he asked. 'Why were you crying?'

'No reason.'

'You've never been a girl who cries for no reason.'

The treacherous finger was tracing a line down her nose now, and then around her lips. Inside Morgan desire stirred. *Fool*, she told herself.

'Why?' Jason asked again.

'It's not important.'

'It is to me. Wait here a moment, Morgan.'

'Why?'

He didn't answer. Feeling a little dazed, she saw him go to the Jeep and drive it to the side of the road. In a minute he was at her window once more.

'Just making sure that nobody will drive into the Jeep—not that there's ever much traffic on this road. Move over, Morgan.'

'Wh-what do you mean?'

'Let me into the car.'

'No, I have to be on my way.' Her voice shook. 'Goodbye, Jason.'

'Please move over.'

'I can't.' A capricious tear rolled down Morgan's cheek. 'It's getting late. You don't seem to understand.'

'Maybe there are things we both don't understand.'

And then his hand moved lower. Before Morgan could react Jason had unlocked the door and then opened it.

'Now will you move over, Morgan?'

'Oh, very well,' she said, trying to sound cross and not quite succeeding. 'But only because I can't drive while you insist on holding the door.'

She slid across the seat, and Jason climbed in beside her. The car, small at the best of times, felt even smaller with Jason in it. He was so big—so powerful—that he dominated every inch of space. His arm touched Morgan's—deliberately, she thought—and a leg rested

just an inch from hers. Her eyes were drawn to his muscled calves, and suddenly she was flooded with memories. She felt dizzy as she tried to push them from her
mind.

'I'll park your car at the side too, Morgan.'

Jason seemed determined to talk to her. That being
the case, she might as well listen.

When her car was also parked at the side of the road
Morgan said, 'Vera drove by just before you did.'

'That's right.' There was amusement in Jason's voice.
'Short visit.'

'We'd finished our discussion.'

'So quickly? Vera…' It was very difficult to say the
words. 'She wants to come back to you, Jason. To…to
be your wife again. To live at the ranch.'

'So she said.'

Morgan's head swung around. 'You couldn't have
discussed things—whatever arrangements are necessary—in such a short time.'

A smile warmed Jason's eyes. 'There wasn't much to
discuss, Morgan.'

'I don't understand…'

'Don't you? It takes two to agree to marriage.'

It was a few seconds before the words made an impact
on Morgan's shocked mind. When they did hope flared
suddenly.

'You mean…? You're saying…?' She couldn't finish
the questions.

Jason answered them anyway. 'I said no to Vera. No
marriage—at least not to her.' Once more the wicked
finger touched her face. 'You look surprised.'

'I thought that since…well, since she wants you…'

'It does take two, Morgan.'

'She talked to me. She…she said you were hurt when
she left you. Well, of course, I knew that was true—
you'd told me so yourself when I first came to the
ranch.'

'And you imagined that because she'd decided to come back to me I'd jump at the offer? That's what Vera thought, Morgan, but you can't be as naïve as all that.'

'Was I being naïve?'

'Yes, my darling. You of all people knew that things had changed.'

Jason was saying things without quite saying them. And Morgan was beginning to feel quite absurdly happy.

An arm went around her shoulders. 'You know that since that night in Austin I haven't been able to keep my hands off you.'

A flush warmed her cheeks. 'I know *that*.'

'Well, then?'

'I know there's an attraction.'

'What a funny way of putting it.' Jason laughed softly. 'An exceedingly strong attraction.'

'But I thought…'

'What did you think, darling?'

'That it was only physical.'

He laughed again and the hand tightened its hold, bringing her closer against him. 'I won't deny that my blood heats any time I'm near you, and that I can't wait to get you in my bed.'

She turned her head away from him, fixing her eyes on the view beyond the window. 'Then I was right.'

'No, my darling, you weren't. Physical attraction is just one aspect of what people feel for each other when they're in love.'

In love… Morgan's heart skipped a beat.

Jason's other hand went to her chin. When he turned her head round to face him she didn't have the will to resist him.

'That's better,' he told her. 'I want to look at your face when we talk. There was something you said, Morgan.'

'What was that?' He was so close to her that she could

see the golden lights in his eyes, and feel his breath on her cheeks.

'Before you drove off.' His voice was suddenly husky. 'You said you loved me, Morgan.'

Her lips quivered. 'I did say that…'

'Words said in the heat of the moment? Because you were angry? Or did you mean it?' His hand was cupping her face now, his thumb brushing slowly up and down her cheek and awakening familiar fires deep inside her. 'I have to know, Morgan.'

What gave him the right to ask her questions when he had never told her how he felt?

'Morgan? Tell me, darling.'

His tone was urgent and his eyes unguarded. His expression was so naked that Morgan shivered.

'Darling—please?'

'I meant it,' Morgan said.

A shudder ran through the tough male body. And then Jason was gathering Morgan against him—no mean feat in the small car, but somehow he managed.

'Morgan,' he said raggedly. 'My darling Morgan.'

They sat silently for a while with their bodies close together, Morgan savouring the hardness of Jason's throat against her cheek. Presently she looked up at him.

'You know how I feel about you…' She stopped.

'You know how I feel about you too.' He looked down at her. 'Don't you, darling?' And when she didn't answer he said, 'Morgan, my lovely Morgan, how can you *not* know? I love you so much. You're everything that makes my life worthwhile.'

Her heart was beating madly in her chest now. She couldn't believe the things he was saying. 'I didn't know. This last week there were times when I thought… But then there was Vera.'

'Bloody woman! Arriving at precisely the wrong time. Almost succeeded in ruining everything.'

'She thought Brent was back and that I'd have gone by now.'

'I know that. Her arrival was no coincidence.'

'You were so angry, Jason. Did you really think I'd poured coffee over her pants?'

'Morgan—'

'I think you should know what happened.'

'No.'

'I want to tell you, Jason.'

'I don't want to hear it. Not a word of it.' His voice was hard now.

Bewildered, Morgan leaned back in his arms. 'If I don't tell you you won't understand.'

'I do understand, darling. Without being told. Not the details, though even those I think I can guess. I shouldn't have questioned you, Morgan.'

Her head turned, and her eyes met his. 'No, Jason, you shouldn't.'

'I should have known instantly, without question, that you would never stoop to doing anything like that. There isn't an ounce of pettiness in you, Morgan. That's one of the things I've learned about you.' His voice grew harder. 'I failed you today, Morgan, and I'll never forgive myself for that. I should have known what had happened. Should have trusted you.'

She looked at him, her eyes shimmering with happiness. No words were necessary. Not any more.

Jason had paused, but now he went on speaking and his voice was troubled. 'That day in Austin, when Vera disturbed us in the condo, she said some terrible things. I expected you to trust me, and you did. You deserve the same kind of trust from me now. Nothing less. *That's* why I don't want you to tell me what happened today. My guess is that Vera was up to one of her nasty little tricks.' A finger touched Morgan's lips as she was about to speak. 'I trust you, my darling. That's all there is to it.'

It was blissful to hear those words—sheer bliss. 'I'm surprised she took off so quickly.'

Jason's expression hardened. 'There was no reason for her to stay once I'd made it clear that there was no future for us. That there was room for only one woman in my life, and that woman wasn't Vera. That I wanted her to leave—quickly, so that I could go after you—and not bother us ever again.'

'She understood?'

'Oh, yes, she won't be back.'

'You seem glad about that. Jason, there's something I don't understand.'

'About Vera?'

'Yes. You must have loved her once.'

'No,' he said flatly. 'I never loved her.'

'You married her.'

'Because I was lonely. Because she made me feel that we could have a life together. For a while I believed her. It's true that I was hurt when she left, but it was my pride that was hurt more than anything else. And in case you're wondering how I could have been attracted to such a vicious woman in the first place—Vera can be very charming when she chooses, Morgan.'

'I'm sure she can,' Morgan said slowly.

A hand slid through her hair, the fingers weaving through the soft strands. 'Time to talk about us, darling. I adore you, Morgan. Your sweetness, your lovely smile. Your face, every inch of your sexy figure.'

Her heart was in her eyes as she looked at him. 'Why didn't you tell me?'

'I planned to,' Jason said ruefully. 'In my own time. Tomorrow evening, if you must know.'

'I don't understand.'

'I was waiting for Brent to get back. As it happens, Vera was waiting for him too and our agendas collided.'

'What does Brent have to do with it, Jason?'

'What I had to say, my darling. I thought I'd wait until your job here was finished.'

'And all the time I thought you couldn't wait to get rid of me. Whenever you mentioned Brent's return you were so cheerful. There were times when I felt like strangling you, Jason.'

'I'm glad you didn't.' Jason nuzzled his lips against Morgan's soft throat. 'And I'm glad I caught up with you while you were still on the ranch, but it wouldn't have mattered if I hadn't. I'd have found you, darling—I wouldn't have rested till I did.'

Morgan smiled mischievously. It was easy to tease Jason now. 'I don't know if I believe you. You wanted me gone, couldn't wait to get rid of me. You said so often enough.'

'Only because I saw you as a threat,' Jason said ruefully. Without loosening his hold on her, he lifted his head. 'You descended on me without any warning—the most beautiful woman I'd ever seen. I knew right away that if you stayed I'd be lost. That you'd turn my world around and that nothing would ever be the same again. And then you'd leave, taking my heart with you.

'I'd been hurt once—by a shallow, selfish woman—but, contrary to what Vera thought, I did get over her. I knew very quickly that you were different, Morgan, and that if I loved you it would be for ever. I didn't want you to hurt me; I didn't want to fall in love with you.'

'Is that why you tried so hard to get rid of me?'

'The only reason, darling. I didn't count on your stubbornness, your absolute refusal to leave the ranch.' He laughed softly. 'Nor on the fact that I would be totally unable to resist you.'

The things he was saying! Words she had heard in her dreams, but had never imagined that she'd hear in real life.

'Remember when you thought I was seducing the cowboys?'

'I was jealous, Morgan.'

'Then you do know that I wasn't after any of them?'

'I do now. There were times when I wasn't sure. Those delectable swimsuit pictures. I was furious when I thought you'd taken them to the cookhouse to excite the men. I should have known better, of course; should have known you wouldn't do that. But that's what jealousy can do to a person, my darling. Even when I found out that Hank had been searching through your things I was still angry.'

'Why, Jason?'

He was silent a few minutes. When he spoke at last his tone was sombre. 'I couldn't stand the thought that other men were looking at your beautiful body.'

'They were only pictures, Jason.' But she thought she knew what he was trying to say.

'I knew by then that I was in love with you, Morgan, and I wanted you for myself. I saw Hank's lips on the pictures of the woman I was crazy about—and I was ready to tear him apart.'

'Your best cowboy,' she said ruefully.

'I couldn't let him stay after that—apart from the fighting. It was Hank or you, Morgan, and the choice was never in question.' Once more he paused. 'I hated the other guy too. The one in the picture.'

'Damian? You had no reason to be jealous of him.'

'The way he was holding you.'

'He was as bored as I was.'

'I don't believe he was bored. Not when he had the loveliest woman in the world in his arms.'

'We were both just doing our jobs, Jason. There was nothing spontaneous about it. It took hours to get just that pose.'

'Hours?'

Her cheeks reddened once more, but her eyes remained steady. '*We* don't need hours, darling.' How wonderful the word sounded on her lips. 'Anything we do together happens because we want it to.'

'I'd like it to happen *now*.' Jason groaned as he pulled Morgan closer. 'If only your car wasn't so small.'

Small it might be, but it didn't stop him from kissing her—a kiss that quickly became hard and passionate.

'Have to stop before I get carried away,' he said after a few minutes. 'Have to get you back to the house.'

'You're forgetting that I was heading the other way.' Morgan's teasing hid her excitement.

'You are going nowhere, my darling. At least not until I've asked you the question I was going to ask you to-morrow. I had it all planned, my darling Morgan—can-dles, wine, soft music. The only thing I don't have is a ring. I thought you might like to choose that.'

'So hard to believe…'

Jason grinned at her. 'Everything was planned, Morgan. It was to be the most romantic evening of our lives. But—because of Vera—here I am, asking the most important question of my life in a car that's too small for a cowboy to stretch his legs.'

Morgan's heart was beating harder than ever now. 'I still haven't heard the question,' she said unsteadily.

His lips were just an inch from hers. 'Will you marry me, Morgan? Will you be my wife?'

'Yes, darling, yes!'

After a rapturous kiss he said, 'You'll make me the happiest man in the world.'

'Oh, Jason,' she said on a sob.

'You're crying again, darling.'

Morgan laughed through her tears. 'That's what hap-piness does to women sometimes.'

'I'm going to make you even happier. I'll do my best to make you the happiest woman ever,' he promised.

'I am already.'

'There's something I have to tell you.' His voice changed. 'I know I can't expect you to give up the life you're used to—can't expect you to be happy for ever on a ranch. And so—'

'Jason!' she interrupted. 'What on earth are you saying?'

'The reason I kept telling you to leave Six-Gate Corral was because I couldn't see a future for us. Couldn't see you ever wanting to live with me here. And so… So this is what I propose. We'll move to Austin. You'll be able to work, and I'll run the ranch from there.'

Morgan was dazed as she looked at Jason, unable to believe the things she was hearing.

'What do you say, Morgan?'

'No, Jason, no! I would never ask you to do that. We'll live here, darling, at Six-Gate Corral.'

'You haven't given yourself time to think about it.' It was Jason's turn to look dazed.

'I don't have to think,' Morgan said vehemently. 'I can't believe you'd dream of making such a sacrifice.'

'It wouldn't be a sacrifice,' he said raggedly, 'because it would mean spending my life with you. That's all that matters to me, Morgan. Living with you is more important than the ranch.'

Morgan had never been more moved. She nuzzled her lips against Jason's throat for a moment, then said, 'Thank you for the offer, my darling, but this will be our home.'

Jason's arms tightened. 'You really mean that?'

'Six-Gate Corral,' Morgan said firmly. 'The only home I'll ever want.'

'Won't you miss your glamorous job, Morgan?'

She shook her head. 'I enjoyed my job, but I'm ready to move on.'

'It will be lonely on the ranch sometimes,' Jason warned.

'How can I be lonely when I'm with you, darling? Besides, I love this life—just as my grandfather loved it. And, more than anything, I love you.'

'Morgan. My lovely Morgan.'

Her head came up and a mischievous sparkle appeared in her eyes. 'There is one thing, though.'

'Name it.'

'I want to be able to ride whenever I feel like it.'

'Of course.'

'Alone, Jason—if that's what I want.'

His eyes darkened. 'You know how I feel about that.'

'Unchaperoned,' she persisted.

'Morgan—'

'I can't have all my movements restricted. I have to have my freedom, Jason. Cowboy's granddaughter—remember? It's important to me, darling. Really important.'

Jason hesitated only a second. 'If it's important to you, my darling, then it's important to me too. Ride whenever you wish—you'll never be accountable to me. Just promise me one thing—be careful. I couldn't bear it if anything happened to you.'

'Nothing will. Oh, Jason!' Her eyes were radiant.

He cupped her face in his hands. 'When can we be married, darling?'

'Soon,' Morgan whispered.

'Very soon,' he said fervently.

He kissed her again, tenderly this time. 'I'll come back for the Jeep later. I'm not a patient man, darling, and all I want now is to get back to the house. I want to make love to you—passionately, properly—and I can't do it in this tiny car.'

A few cows raised startled heads as the car sped by. The two people inside, sitting close together, didn't notice them. As the ranch-house came into sight there was only one thing on their minds.

MILLS & BOON®

Next Month's Romances

Each month you can choose from a wide variety of romance novels from Mills & Boon. Below are the new titles to look out for next month from the Presents™ and Enchanted™ series.

Presents™

THE PERFECT SEDUCTION	Penny Jordan
A NANNY NAMED NICK	Miranda Lee
INDISCRETIONS	Robyn Donald
SCANDALOUS BRIDE	Diana Hamilton
SATISFACTION GUARANTEED	Helen Brooks
FLETCHER'S BABY!	Anne McAllister
THE VENGEFUL GROOM	Sara Wood
WILLING TO WED	Cathy Williams

Enchanted™

LOVE CAN WAIT	Betty Neels
THE YOUNGEST SISTER	Anne Weale
BREAKFAST IN BED	Ruth Jean Dale
THE ONLY SOLUTION	Leigh Michaels
OUTBACK BRIDE	Jessica Hart
RENT-A-COWBOY	Barbara McMahon
TO MARRY A STRANGER	Renee Roszel
HAUNTED SPOUSE	Heather Allison

MILLS & BOON®

Medical Romance™

*Don't miss Josie Metcalfe's wonderfully
heartwarming trilogy...*

St Augustine's Hospital

*We know you'll love getting to know
this fascinating group of friends*

FIRST THINGS FIRST
Nick and Polly's story
in October

SECOND CHANCE
Wolff and Laura's story
in November

THIRD TIME LUCKY
Leo and Hannah's story
in January

St Augustine's: where love surprises everyone

FOUR FREE
specially selected
Enchanted™ novels
<u>PLUS</u> a FREE Mystery Gift
when you return this page...

Return this coupon and we'll send you 4 Mills & Boon® Enchanted™ novels and a
mystery gift absolutely FREE! We'll even pay the postage and packing for you.

We're making you this offer to introduce you to the benefits of the Reader Service™–
FREE home delivery of brand-new Mills & Boon Enchanted novels, at least a
month before they are available in the shops, FREE gifts and a monthly Newsletter
packed with information, competitions, author profiles and lots more...

Accepting these FREE books and gift places you under no obligation to buy, you
may cancel at any time, even after receiving just your free shipment. Simply
complete the coupon below and send it to:

MILLS & BOON READER SERVICE, FREEPOST, CROYDON, SURREY, CR9 3WZ.

READERS IN EIRE PLEASE SEND COUPON TO PO BOX 4546, DUBLIN 24

NO STAMP NEEDED

Yes, please send me 4 free Enchanted novels and a mystery gift.
I understand that unless you hear from me, I will receive 6 superb new titles
every month for just £2.20* each, postage and packing free. I am under no
obligation to purchase any books and I may cancel or suspend my subscription
at any time, but the free books and gift will be mine to keep in any case.
(I am over 18 years of age)

N7YE

Ms/Mrs/Miss/Mr_____
BLOCK CAPS PLEASE

Address_____

_____

_____ Postcode _____

DEBBIE MACOMBER

THIS MATTER OF MARRIAGE

Hallie McCarthy gives herself a year to find Mr Right. Meanwhile, her handsome neighbour is busy trying to win his ex-wife back. As the two compare notes on their disastrous campaigns, each finds the perfect partner lives right next door!

"In the vein of When Harry Met Sally, Ms Macomber will delight."

—Romantic Times

AVAILABLE IN PAPERBACK FROM SEPTEMBER 1997

MILLS & BOON®

Back by Popular Demand

COLLECTOR'S EDITION

A collector's edition of favourite titles from one of Mills & Boon's best-loved romance authors.

Don't miss this wonderful collection of sought-after titles, now reissued in beautifully matching volumes and presented as one cherished collection.

Look out next month for:

Title #3   Charade in Winter
Title #4   A Fever in the Blood

Available wherever Mills & Boon books are sold

Meet
A PERFECT FAMILY

Shocking revelations and heartache lie just beneath the surface of their charmed lives.

The Crightons are a family in conflict. Long-held resentments and jealousies are reawakened when three generations gather for a special celebration.

One revelation leads to another - a secret war-time liaison, a carefully concealed embezzlement scam, the illicit seduction of another's wife. The façade begins to crack, revealing a family far from perfect, underneath.

"Women everywhere will find pieces of themselves in Jordan's characters"
–Publishers Weekly

The coupon is valid only in the UK and Eire against purchases made in retail outlets and not in conjunction with any Reader Service or other offer.

50p OFF
COUPON
VALID UNTIL: 31.12.1997

PENNY JORDAN'S *A PERFECT FAMILY*

9 904170 210508 >

0472 00195